PRAISE FOR LEE McCLAIN AND MY ALTERNATE LIFE!

"Witty, dramatic, well paced, a page turner. Trinity stands up and lives on the page: gutsy, vulnerable, street-smart, people-smart— okay, just plain smart, a survivor with a heart."
—Nancy Springer, Edgar Award–winning author of *I Am Mordred*

CONFRONTING THE PAST

"I'm not a telemarketer," I said quickly. "I'm calling you, just you."

"Do I know you from somewhere?" the woman asked. "Your voice sounds familiar."

I had a hard time catching my breath, and my throat seemed to close. Inside of me, so many words fought to get out.

Yes, you know me, I'm the daughter you gave away!

MY ALTERNATE *LIFE*

LEE McCLAIN

SMOOCH NEW YORK CITY

SMOOCH ®

September 2004

Published by

Dorchester Publishing Co., Inc.
200 Madison Avenue
New York, NY 10016

ISBN 0-8439-5451-5

The name "SMOOCH" and its logo are trademarks of Dorchester Publishing Co., Inc.

Printed in the United States of America.

Visit us on the web at www.smoochya.com.

ACKNOWLEDGMENTS

I couldn't have finished this book without my wonderful critique partners and writing advisers: Leslie Davis Guccione, Tory LeBlanc, Felicia Mason, Nancy Springer, and Moni Thompson. Much appreciation also goes to Dennis Jerz, who taught me the basics of computer gaming. Special thanks to my amazing daughter, Gracie, and my smart and practical husband, Mike; you are my inspiration and my support.

MY ALTERNATE
LIFE

Chapter One

I didn't plan to jump out of a moving car. And I definitely didn't plan to land in a cow pie.

It's just that Fred wasn't listening when I said I really, really, really didn't want a new family.

Fred's streaky gray hair flowed down the back of his tie-dyed shirt, and his voice was classic social worker. "There's your new high school," he said. "It's small. Homey. You'll make friends fast."

But I saw the squat, light-brick building a different way. Small schools are cliquish and nosy, and there's not a lot of space for difference.

And I, Trinity B. Jones, am different.

Not to mention that I'm totally urban. So when I saw the field full of cows right next to the school, I lost it and jumped.

Fortunately, I was wearing my leather jacket and jeans, so I didn't get scraped up by the strands of barbed wire I flew through. And I'm not totally stupid—I grabbed Fred's cell beforehand. My plan was to call Nate, my boyfriend back in the city where I so fully belonged, and get him to beg, borrow, or steal a car and come rescue me.

The cow pie gunked up my plans. "Euew!" I screamed and knelt there in the tall grass, trying to wipe off my jacket. It was the most expensive thing I owned. A gift from Nate.

Behind me I could hear Fred's old Ford screeching to a halt.

"Are you okay?" asked a girl's voice above me.

I looked up to see a line of girls dressed in workout clothes. They were leaning over the fence that separated the school from the cow pasture, squinting in the late-afternoon sun.

Fred came panting up behind me. "Trinity B. Jones," he said, "what do you think you're doing? You could have been killed, and just when—" He squatted down in the tall grass beside me. "Are you all right?"

"I'm fine," I said, "but my jacket isn't. They need to curb their cows around here."

"She landed in cow crap!" giggled one of the girls.

"Don't talk trash," said another girl.

I rolled my eyes. If that was trash talk, this place was even more backward than I'd thought.

"Trinity," Fred said, taking hold of my clean

arm, "get back in the car. You know I'll have to write an incident report about this."

"And get me sent to Saint Helen's?" I asked. *That would be cool.* Saint Helen's Home for Girls was in the same neighborhood as my old foster family, which meant the same neighborhood as Nate.

"In your dreams," Fred said. "Come on, back in the car."

"Flag Team! Line up! Competition is one week away!" came a voice behind the line of girls.

I sighed and headed back toward the car, letting Fred fuss with a little scrape on my knuckle while I used his bandanna to wipe off my smelly jacket.

After we were inside, Fred started driving again, but he was at least taking me more seriously. "Trinity, listen to me. This family is perfect for you. What's more, Susan is interested in adopting you, if everything works out well."

"Yeah, right." I knew that would never happen, not at my age. I'd been to enough adoption picnics to know that adoptive parents wanted a cute little baby to hold, not a fifteen-year-old with brown skin, a 34-C, and a nose ring.

"I thought you liked Susan." Fred cut off the main road and turned right in between two fields. A pickup truck drove by and the driver gave us a little wave. Three fingers, toot-toot of his horn. Where I was from, that would have been a gang signal.

"Susan's fine," I said. "It's not that."

"She thinks you're more than fine," he said. "She's very impressed with your academic achievements and she thinks she has a lot to offer you. She's a lawyer, you know."

"Yeah, big deal." My regular social worker had already given me the lowdown on how Susan worked a lot in family court, and that was why she got interested in foster care. Susan had come into the city to meet me a couple of times. She was a real businesswoman, all suits and sensible shoes, and she talked smart. Nice enough. But I didn't want to be her good deed for the year.

We were getting closer to the house; I could tell from how Fred turned onto another, even narrower road.

My heart started pounding harder. This was really going to happen and I didn't want it to. I just wanted Nate, so he could wrap his big arms around me and tell me everything would be okay.

But there was something else I wanted even more, and because I was pushed into a corner, I blurted it out. "I don't want a new family, I want my real mom."

Fred glanced over at me. "Trinity, that's not going to happen."

"Why not? If she knew the Holmsteads put us all out on the street, she'd take me." The Holmsteads had been my foster parents for five years. It was nothing great, but it wasn't bad.

4

Fred shook his head. "She couldn't take care of you. She would want nothing more than for us to find you a permanent adoptive family." He turned into a long dirt driveway.

We approached a big white house. The front porch had rocking chairs and a swing. A couple of big trees stood in the yard, and an old Volvo was parked beside the house.

Balloons bobbed on the front porch railing and a computer-generated banner read, "Welcome, Trinity!"

That made me feel funny. Sort of happy, in the babyish part of myself, because I'd never had birthday parties and all that, and when I was a kid, I'd really wanted to.

But it also seemed kind of fake. Susan didn't know me and she didn't know how it was all going to work out, so why act like everything's beautiful?

And the front door was opening, and there was Susan, plus a teenage girl about my age. Oh, yeah, her *real* daughter. She'd been too busy with all her social activities to meet me when Susan had.

They were both smiling and waving.

I felt like I might get sick. Everything was moving along faster than the race car video games Nate and I loved to play. But I was going in the wrong direction: away from what I wanted, and toward what I didn't want.

Fred stopped the car but, thankfully, he didn't

open the door right away. He turned to look at me. "You okay, kiddo?" he asked.

I had to swallow a couple of times before I could answer. "No."

"Look," he said, reaching into his shirt pocket. "Before we go in, I have something for you. It might make you feel better about everything." He handed me an envelope.

"Thanks." I was surprised. He'd only taken over my case a month ago. And in a whole long string of social workers, not one had ever given me a gift. I hoped it was money. "Can I open it now?"

A funny smile crinkled his face, and a sparkle in his eyes made him look like a mad little elf. "No, wait until later, when you're on the computer," he said.

By the time "later" came, my head was spinning. Maybe it was the cake Susan had made—super sweet, yellow with chocolate icing, my favorite. Someone must have told her.

It was nice of her to make it and I managed to choke some down, but I was uptight. For one thing, the daughter, Kelly, wasn't exactly my type. She was skinny and tailored and tense. But Susan clearly thought that, since we were both fifteen, we were going to be the best of friends.

"Now, you each have your own bedroom," Susan said, upstairs, after Fred had left and we'd brought in all my stuff. "You share the study and bathroom."

My bedroom looked like the set of *City Girls Go Country*: hardwood floors, fringy little rugs, and ruffled curtains tied back with yellow ribbons.

I could tell Susan had decorated it and wanted me to gush. Well, tough. Sure, I was grateful to have my own room. But this place totally wasn't me.

I was chrome and black leather, not flowers and country charm. Just more evidence that this wasn't the right place for me.

When I saw the computer in the study, I brightened up. While I was here, until I came up with a new plan, at least I could stay in touch with my old friends. "I need to check my email," I said.

"I need the computer tonight, too," Kelly said quickly. "Homework."

"I'm sure you two can negotiate that," Susan said. "Kelly, you've got laundry in the basement to fold and put away, and Trinity, you need to get your things organized for school tomorrow."

"Whoa," I said. "Wait up. I can't start school tomorrow."

"Why not?" Susan's eyebrows went up just a little.

Because I'm freaking out here. "I, um, I'm not registered. Don't I have to do some official stuff first?"

"I've got it all taken care of," Susan said. "I'll go in with you tomorrow and we'll finalize your classes, but that's it. You should be able to start with your homeroom period and go through the day."

"Mom's efficient," Kelly said.

I excused myself, went into the bright pink bathroom I was to share with Kelly, and threw up.

When I came back out and went into my bedroom, Susan was waiting. "Are you okay?" she asked.

I nodded. "I just haven't been feeling all that great. Maybe I have a little flu. Maybe I shouldn't go to school tomorrow."

Susan patted the bed beside her and I sat down, keeping a good foot of distance between us. I could tell she wanted to put her arm around me, but no matter what her title was, she wasn't my mother. And I wasn't staying. So there was no point in getting all lovey-dovey.

"Trinity," she said, "I know this must be very difficult for you, leaving your old home and starting out new."

"It's okay," I lied.

Obviously, she didn't believe me. "Even though it's hard, I want you to go to school tomorrow unless you're really sick. We believe in good school attendance in this family."

I stared down at my knees. I wasn't really sick, but I dreaded the thought of starting out new, in the middle of tenth grade, at some school where everyone already had their friends.

"Kelly will help you get through the day," she said, "and we'll make sure you know your way around. It's a small school, so I think you'll find it a lot friendlier than what you're used to."

"Sure." I could tell there was no use arguing with Susan. After all, she was a lawyer.

Anyway, it was only for a few days, just long enough for me to come up with a plan. I could stand anything for a few days.

"Good girl." She scooted over and gave me a little squeeze around the shoulders.

I went into my fence-post act. No way was I hugging her back.

She stood up. "Now, I'll bet you can get on that computer before Kelly comes back up."

The thought of e-mailing Nate made me smile. "Thanks," I said, and meant it.

Moments later I was online, and just as I'd hoped, there was an e-mail from Nate.

Hey, babe, I miss you, want you, love you. Scope the scene and tell me when, I'll snag a car and come visit. It's not the same around here without you.

I wrapped my arms around my middle as I read it again and again. Nate wasn't much of a talker but he was sincere and he had respect. We'd been together for a year and before I left, we swore we'd stay faithful to each other.

I answered e-mails from some other friends and surfed a little. Kelly wasn't back and I figured she was talking to her mom. I didn't feel tired, more like high-strung and worried, and I didn't know what to do with myself. Then I remembered the card old Fred had given me. I got it out and opened it.

The card itself looked like Fred, with a swirled design and a cosmic poem inside. No money, unfortunately.

Fred's message said, "If you ever feel like going home, check out this site." And there was a Web address.

Oh, geez. Probably some psychological site for unhappy teens. But what the hey, I qualified for that! I typed in the address: *www.ALTLIVES.com.*

What came up was a game. Some gift! I mean, I know social workers don't make much money, but to tell me he's giving me a gift and then point me to a Web site with some silly computer game . . . oh, well. Fred wasn't the first social worker to disappoint me.

Just for fun, I started playing.

The first prompt was *A car shows up in your driveway. Fred's driving.*

You:

I'd played a few old-fashioned games like this before: a lot of text, kind of boring. But because the name was Fred, I wondered if old Fred was involved in making up this game. So I played along. What would I do if Fred showed up in my driveway?

GET IN, I typed.

Fred starts driving. Where do you want to go?

You: TELL HIM I WANT TO GO BACK TO THE CITY.

Fred drives.

There was some la-di-da stuff about driving past cows and horses, just like when Fred and I had come out here, which was weird. But I answered all the questions.

Once we got to the city, the game asked me where I wanted to go. I thought about it.

Did I really want to go back to the Holmsteads? After they'd gotten sick of fostering teenagers and kicked us all out?

And anyway it was just a game. I figured that once I got as specific as a single address, it wouldn't work anymore.

But what the heck. I was getting bored with the game. I typed in Nate's address.

Are you sure? the computer asked.

I blinked.

YES, I'M SURE.

As you approach Nate's house, you see him coming out. What do you do?

HUG HIM! I typed.

You're still in the car.

II

Oh, duh. I typed, GET OUT OF THE CAR.

He doesn't see you because he's talking to someone.

WHO IS HE TALKING TO?

Jessica and Tanika.

I stared at the screen as my stomach knotted up. This was truly bizarre. I knew Jessica and Tanika. They were twins. And they'd been hot for Nate as long as I could remember.

I DON'T BELIEVE YOU.

For, like, ten seconds, a visual flashed on the screen. Sure enough, it was the front of Nate's house. Jessica and Tanika each had one of his hands, and they were pulling him down his front porch steps as he laughed and tried to resist, but not very hard.

Chapter Two

My stomach hurt and my heart pounded. I felt like logging off.

What a stupid game. What a creepy game. I knew it wasn't real; I knew Nate wouldn't even be talking to those twin tarts, but it still bothered me.

Fred had given me a sadistic game. What was up with that?

And it made some tiny corner of my heart question: Would Nate really be faithful to me, now that I was gone?

What do you want to do now? the game asked.

I was disgusted with it. SCRATCH THEIR EYES OUT?

You cannot interact at this level.

Yeah, whatever. All of a sudden I got an idea. Before I could think, I typed it in: I WANT TO SEE MY MOTHER.

In no way did I think the game would do something like that. I didn't even know if my mom was still in Pittsburgh, although that's where we'd always lived. She could be anywhere.

But the game made Fred start driving me. He drove out of Nate's street on the South Side, crossing the river on a bridge I recognized and then passing neighborhoods I didn't know.

My heart was really pounding now. Ever since Mom had that bad time when I was eight and gave me up, I'd wanted to see her again, but all I got from my social workers were excuses. It made me wonder: Was there something really wrong with Mom? Was she sick? Dead?

And was I supposed to believe that now I could see her because of some stupid game? Some really weird, bizarre, scary game?

A tap on my shoulder made me jump, violently. It was Kelly. "Could you get off now?" she asked. "I've been waiting for, like, half an hour."

"In a minute," I said.

"I need the computer now."

"Too bad. You can wait five minutes."

She actually reached around and tried to restart the computer. I shoved her hand away, but she grabbed the mouse and held it where I couldn't reach. "It's *my* computer."

I put on a sad face to make her think she'd won, then jumped for the mouse and shoved her hard at the same time. As I turned back to the computer I heard a crash behind me. But I didn't pay attention, because the game said we were approaching my mother's house.

I WANT TO SEE HER, I typed.

Are you sure?

I thought of what I'd seen with Nate. I wished I hadn't. Was I going to see something I didn't like about Mom?

But the pull in my heart to see her again was so great that I typed YES after only a slight hesitation.

Again, it was that video flash, low quality.

And there she was.

I dashed away the tears that sprang to my eyes and leaned closer, trying to see. There was some kind of party going on. The surroundings were fancier than I'd expected; in fact, it looked like everyone was wearing suits and sequined dresses.

My mother stood in the middle of a group of admiring people, mostly men. And why not? She was the prettiest person there. She was laughing and talking and seemed to be having a great time.

So she wasn't sick or dead. She looked to be fine. Better than fine.

My throat was all choked up. I wanted to go and bury myself in her arms. At the same time, I was wondering: How could she be so happy when she'd given away her daughter? Did she know I'd been put out and had to find a new family in the sticks?

I WANT TO TALK TO HER, I typed.

The video flashed off. *You cannot interact at this level.*

I WANT TO SEE HER AGAIN.

Two hands clamped down on my shoulders. It was Susan. "Kelly says you hit her and knocked her down," she said.

"I'm sorry," I muttered. "This is important." As I said it I shrunk the screen, because I didn't want Susan to catch on to what I was doing. I didn't trust her.

"You need to get off the computer now and apologize to Kelly," she said. "We don't hit each other in this family."

"I didn't mean to," I said quickly, "and I'll just be another minute."

"You'll get off right now," she said, and hit control-alt-delete to restart the computer.

"Oh, man!" Like mother, like daughter. Control-alt-delete freaks.

"And you won't be on again for a week. Trinity, there are consequences for hitting and disobeying in this house."

I felt my eyes narrow into the mean look that Mrs. Holmstead said gave her the creeps. A week. Well, I'd just have to find another computer. Because I was going to play the game, see my mother again, and talk to her.

I was going to find a way to go home.

* * *

The next morning, things went from bad to worse.

It wasn't just that Kelly hogged the bathroom; I'd expected that. I'd spent my teenage years up till now in a big foster family, so I knew to set my alarm early and get my shower.

Kelly had been an only child all her life. She'd always had her own bathroom. So she was deeply offended by seeing a couple of my hairs in the sink and by the fact that I'd used her shampoo.

She went crying to her mother, prejudicing her against me again this morning. When I came downstairs in my normal school clothes, Susan freaked out.

"Trinity, you are not wearing a studded dog collar for your first day of school. I draw the line there," she said.

"It's the style." I scanned the boxes of healthy breakfast cereals out on the kitchen counter, looking for something to eat. "Do you guys have any Sugar Bears or Honeycomb? Anything sweet?"

"You don't need food like that," Kelly said from behind a bowl of strawberries.

I tried, I really tried, to keep my voice pleasant. "What's that supposed to mean?"

She gave my backside a pointed glare. "If those jeans get any tighter, you'll split the seams."

I spun and grabbed her shoulder. "You sayin' I'm fat, prom queen?"

"Mom!"

"Oh, geez." I let go of her and rolled my eyes.

Susan turned away from the Crock-Pot she'd been filling with weird-looking vegetables. "Kelly, stop whining about everything Trinity does. Trinity, take off that collar."

"But I like my collar," I said. "My boyfriend gave it to me."

"Doesn't that just show what he thinks of you." Kelly's voice was snotty.

There was no way she'd get away with insulting my man. I started toward her.

Susan walked in between us, pushing us apart. "Kelly, go upstairs and finish getting ready. We're leaving in five minutes. Trinity, believe it or not, I do have your best interests at heart. Leather and studs are not on the 'make a good first impression' list at Linden High, neither with teachers nor students."

"I don't care what impression I make," I said. It was true. I was just in this cow-patch school temporarily, until I could get back to the city. Back to Nate. And even more importantly, back to the place I now knew was within driving distance of my real mom.

Susan lifted her eyes to the ceiling like she thought she might find some help up there. "Choose your battles, Susan," she said to herself in a quiet, prissy voice.

Geez, why didn't she just yell at me or back-hand me or something? What was she, a wimp?

My thoughts must have shown on my face, because she glared at me. "All right, wear it. But don't say I didn't warn you."

When Kelly and I walked into the crowd of students before the first bell, I almost wished I'd listened to Susan.

"Eeeek! It's the cow pie girl!" screamed a cheerleader type who was obviously one of the group that had seen my car-jump the previous afternoon.

"What's that around her neck?" asked a red-headed guy.

"Kelly! Do you know her?" another girl asked.

They were all dressed in clothes that were so five minutes ago, and they talked about me like I wasn't even there. And, just as I'd suspected, the place was lily-white, making a brown-skinned kid like me stand out even more. I even heard someone whisper, "Is she black, or what?" Probably thrown by my baby blues.

The fact that they couldn't fit me into their neat categories gave me a little satisfaction. The only other good part was how mortified Kelly looked. She'd been assigned, both by Susan and by the school, to help me find my way around on this first day, and she was hating it.

She gave her friends a little wave. "I have to

help Trinity find her classrooms," she said with a look that suggested I was mentally deficient.

"Why don't you tell them I'm your new sister?" I asked just to needle her.

"Look," she hissed as soon as we'd passed through the crowd, "I'm in the running for Fall Queen, and I have a good chance to make it. I don't need you messing up my chances."

"Fall Queen, huh? Do they choose flat-chested girls for stuff like that around here?"

The insult came out without a whole lot of power, more like habit. The truth was, Kelly had a cute, skinny figure a lot of girls would kill for. But to my surprise, her eyes got all shiny with tears.

I didn't know how to handle that. I wanted her to fight back. The way she got all upset made me feel like a real jerk.

We walked in silence to my first class. At the door, she stopped. "Have fun with the geeks," she said. "And you can find your own way to your morning classes."

I found out what she meant about geeks when the bell rang and people came charging into the class. It was AP English and the kids were *not* the winners of the school. What is it about smart kids? Why do they always have such a high proportion of acne, bad hair, and fashion disasters?

The good thing was, it was a computer classroom and the teacher had assigned groups of students to do Internet research on *Hamlet*. I saw a chance to play Fred's game again and try to find out more about my mom.

The bad thing was, the group I had to work with. I'd already picked out a wimpy-looking group of girls I knew I could get the computer from, but the teacher assigned me instead to a group led by an obnoxious nerd in a plaid shirt and thick black glasses.

"Trinity, meet Lonnie, Roland, and Michelle. They'll be your partners for the *Hamlet* project," she said. "Lonnie, I expect you to make Trinity feel welcome."

"We welcome you and your accessories, too," he said with an English accent.

"Lonnie comes from Manchester, England," the teacher said, beaming with her own good idea. "So he's from out of town, too. He'll help you catch up with class work."

"Okay." I looked my group over. Roland looked like a Roland: roly-poly with pale blond hair. Michelle was serious and totally out of style in a flowered knee-length sheath dress, pumps, and pink-framed glasses, but I sort of admired her guts to wear such a getup.

If, in fact, she'd worn it as a conscious choice. With geeks you never knew.

Lonnie, sprawled in a chair, was giving me a once-over that made me nervous.

So I spoke first. "Whaddup, Brit-Boy?"

"I was just wondering," he said, "about the significance of your canine collar."

Why was this collar such a big deal? Back home, half the girls wore them. "It was a gift from someone with twice the *cojones* you have."

He raised his eyebrows. "You only have the data to validate one half of that statement," he said, letting his legs fall apart and glancing downward. "But that could be corrected."

Whoa! I felt myself blushing and I hated it.

"Lonnie, you're disgusting," Michelle said.

"I'm just taking the opportunity to find out why an intelligent woman would willingly wear a symbol of subjugation," he said.

"A symbol of what?" I asked.

"Subjugation. The dog wears a collar so that its master may control its movements. Also, so that everyone knows the identity of the owner."

"Geez," I said, "it's just a necklace. Why does everyone get so bent out of shape about it?" I knew I'd lost the argument, but I told myself it didn't matter. Who cared what these people thought, anyway? If I could get on the computer, I could find out more about my mom and be out of here in days.

Roland was looking at some Web pages about *Hamlet*.

"Hey," I said, "let me give it a try."

"I just want to follow this link to some of the

first productions," he said. "They have old playbills and photos and everything."

"You into drama?" I asked him.

He nodded with a shy smile. Actually, he
looked sort of sweet when he smiled—unlike
Lonnie, who looked like the devil with a dim-
ple—so I restrained myself from making a mean
comment about a fat boy's chances on the stage.
Instead, I smiled back and said, "Look, print your
page and you can come back to it. I really, really
need to be on the computer for a few minutes.
Please?"

"She has to contact her master," Lonnie said.

"Shut up." I typed *www.ALTLIVES.com* into
the address box.

"We're only supposed to use the computer for
the project," said Michelle. "Mrs. Lynch won't let
us work alone if she finds out we're using it for
something else."

"You can blame it on me," I said as the game
came up.

Chapter Three

I WANT TO SEE MY MOTHER AGAIN, I typed. And then I realized that to get more information, I needed to hear what she was saying. Last night the video hadn't had sound. I WANT TO HEAR WHAT SHE'S SAYING.

Choose sound or video, the game responded.

I glanced around. Michelle, Lonnie, and Roland were arguing amongst themselves and, scattered around the computer classroom, other groups were working. The noise level was high, but I knew that a computer's audio would cut through it.

CAN I SEE VIDEO AND GET A TRANSCRIPT OF THE AUDIO?

Either/or.

I'LL TAKE A TRANSCRIPT.

It was some transcript. Just like a play.

*A woman with long brunette hair lounges in
bed, reading the paper.*

That would be my mom. I remembered how
she'd loved to read the paper and magazines in
bed. Every morning, she'd spent hours doing just
that, because she usually worked the late shift.

*Her maid enters and begins picking up
clothes that are scattered around the floor.*

Her maid? How far had Mom come up in the
world, anyway? And if she was so rich, why
hadn't she come to get me?

Maybe she was rich but sick. Maybe she was
waiting for the exact perfect time to invite me
back into her life.

Maybe she was just like the Holmsteads and all
the wannabe adopters at the picnics. Couldn't be
bothered with a troublesome teenager like me.

Maybe she remembered how I'd always gotten in the way of her dates, her job, and her big
plans to rise up in the world.

It sure seemed like she was doing better without me.

*"Look at this!" the woman says, jabbing at
the paper with a long fingernail.*
*The maid comes to her side and examines
the paper.*

"Lydia Hoffman is listed as best-dressed again!" The woman throws the paper on the floor. *"That's the third time this year. I wish, just once, I could win best-dressed at one of these events."*

"The Hoffmans have been in Pittsburgh for a long time," says the maid.

"What, so it's who you know?" The woman swings her legs over the side of the bed. *"Well, I'll tell you what, Mary. I may be new to this part of town, but I can figure out a way to get what I want. And if I want to get photographed for best-dressed in Pittsburgh, then that's what I'll do."*

"I believe you, ma'am."

"You know what, they usually choose either the young, pretty ones or old rich hags like Lydia Hoffman," she says. *"Nobody here knows my age. They all think I'm at least ten years younger than I am. That should help."*

"Did you find that site with the playbills yet, Trinity?" Lonnie asked, coming up behind me. He put his hands over mine on the keyboard, surrounding me with his body, and entered a new Web address into the window.

"Hey, quit it!" I was so disconcerted by how big he felt, his arms around me and his chest right up against my back, that I couldn't stop him in time.

Just like that, my mom was gone.

I spun around and shoved one of his arms away. "What'd you do that for, you big—"

Mrs. Lynch was right there. "Problems, Trinity?" she asked.

"No," I said, stepping hard on Lonnie's foot.

Later, in the lunch line, I didn't even suffer the usual new-kid worries about where I was going to sit and who I'd sit with. I just daydreamed about my mother.

Now I really believed she was surviving and thriving. The transcript this morning was so totally her. She'd always wanted to be some kind of a star, in magazines or on TV. She'd always hoped someone would come into whatever diner she worked at and discover her and sweep her away to a better life.

We'd even believed it was going to happen, too. Right before she got sick and had to give me away, she'd met a rich businessman who'd really seemed interested in her.

I didn't like to think about that time, so I focused back on where I was: the cafeteria, with kids yelling and trays banging and the smell of greasy pizza and overcooked vegetables.

Even though nobody talked to me, they were looking. I could already tell this school didn't have many new kids, from the stares and nudges that had come my way all morning.

At the front of the line, the cafeteria worker smiled at me. "You must be new," she said. "Give me your name, dear. I'm sure you'll be in my computer."

"Trinity B. Jones."

She typed, frowned, shook her head.

"Look," I said, "I probably get the free lunch. My foster mom must have forgotten to register me. I'll tell her tonight."

Around me, though, there was a funny silence, like everyone took a breath at once.

I glanced back at the line. All the kids were staring at me.

Into the silence came a British voice. "There is no such thing as a free lunch, darling."

That broke the tension and everybody laughed.

The cafeteria worker turned red. "Let me just write down your name, honey, and you go on. I'm sure it's fine."

Just then Kelly rushed up, out of breath. "Trinity! There you are." She lowered her voice. "Mom forgot to pay our accounts, so she came back in and gave me the money this morning. Here." She handed me five bucks like it was nothing.

"There, you see?" The cafeteria worker was relieved into perkiness. "Everything's fine." She hurried up and made change.

In the space of time that took, Kelly had started whispering with a couple of other girls in the line. As I walked out into the table area with my tray, looking for a space where I could be by myself, she came up beside me. "Don't you *ever* embarrass me like that again," she said.

I kept walking. "Like what, Fall Queen?"

Her face turned red. "Asking for a free lunch and talking about being a foster kid. What are you thinking?"

I plunked down my tray at the empty end of a table. "If you didn't live in such a podunk town, you'd know that a lot of kids get free lunch."

"Not around here, they don't." She tossed back her hair. "I can't believe all the kids know I'm associated with you. What a disaster."

I could have reassured her by telling her I wouldn't be here long, but I didn't want to make her comfortable life any more comfortable. "Thanks for bailing me out, sis," I said loudly. I took a bite of hamburger, and watched in satisfaction while she huffed away.

"Countdown to Fall Dance, six weeks." The girl who said it was right outside my bathroom stall, and since I was getting bored, I decided to eavesdrop.

I'd been in there for more than half an hour, skipping my math class. I couldn't find it after Kelly ditched me for the afternoon. I needed a break, anyway.

"Did he ask you yet?" another girl shrilled.

"No, but I think he will tonight."

"Did you hear how the planning committee is fighting so much that they might cancel the dance?"

"They'll never do that. They can't!"

Just girl-gab. I let their excited voices fade into the background and went back to thinking about my mom. I was still amazed at what she'd done for herself. Lying around in bed talking to her maid? She must be in heaven.

But she couldn't know that I was in cow pie hell. If she did, she'd come and get me out.

Wouldn't she?

Well, maybe not now, but soon. Maybe she still had a few goals she needed to reach before she took me on again. Maybe she wanted to make sure she was really well set up, with plenty of money.

What she had sure looked to be enough, though.

Something dark and ugly twisted in my stomach. Suddenly I felt about five years old. *Can't get mad at Mommy, don't let her see you're mad, she hates that.*

"There are too many popular girls to know who'll get Queen," said the same girl's voice outside my stall. "But I know who'll get King."

There were sounds of running water. "Who?"

"Josh Johnson."

"Yeah, you're probably right," another voice said. "I hope not, though."

"Why? He's a babe. And he's so funny."

"Yeah," the first girl said, "but he's mean."

They went on talking and I went back to daydreaming. I wanted out of Linden Falls and back into Mom's life. But would she welcome me with open arms?

I forced myself to think about what it would be like if I rang her doorbell, if she introduced me to her husband and friends.

Even back when I was five and six, she sometimes didn't like me to meet her friends. Mom had had me real young, and she looked young, and when people saw me, it aged her.

Also, Mom was white. My dad, not that I'd ever met him, had been black and something else, probably Native American. Mom claimed not to know, but how could she not know? She just hated talking about it.

For all I knew, she hated my color. Or maybe she hated how I didn't have movie star looks like she did.

Would I stand out in her world now, a world that was rich and probably all white? Would she be ashamed of my light brown skin, my super-curly hair, my full lips?

My thoughts were getting to be a drag. And the bathroom and hall sounds were dying down, indicating that the next class was about to begin.

I'd better try to find it, so that I didn't get in trouble for missing the whole day.

I emerged from the stall and realized that the same girls were still talking about the Fall Dance.

"You know," one of them said, "if Josh is going to be King, then it doesn't matter which girl is most popular. The queen'll be whoever Josh asks to the dance."

I was so surprised by that, and so excited by an idea forming inside me, that I lost my cool and spun to face them. "You mean the Fall King and Queen are decided by the couple, not individually?"

She gave me a look. "Yeah."

The idea took form. "Is Josh dating anyone?"

The two of them glanced at each other.

"You're not *too* nosy, are you?" one of them said finally.

Without thinking I took a couple steps closer until I was right in her face. "Just answer the question, honeybunch."

Instead, she backed up real fast, tripped on the trash can, and half fell. "Ow!" She started to cry. "Brittany, get a teacher. She pushed me!"

I rolled my eyes and held out a hand to her. "I didn't push you. You tripped."

"Get away from me!"

The girl named Brittany ran out of the bathroom, and the bell rang. I left, too.

What wimps. Bathroom fights were the norm

where I'd come from, and a little talk and pushing didn't even signify.

Still, I knew I'd get in trouble. I stood out enough that everyone could recognize and describe me.

Despite that, I walked to my next class floating high. Because I'd just figured everything out.

I had to do something to make Mom impressed with me, impressed enough to know I'd be an asset and not a liability. And knowing Mom, I'd just figured out what would impress her.

I had to be Fall Queen.

Now, obviously, that wasn't going to happen by a popularity contest. There was no way a new girl could get inside school cliques in six weeks. Plus all the girls here already hated me.

But the key to being crowned Fall Queen wasn't popularity. Kelly was going about it all wrong.

The sure route was to date the mysterious Josh Johnson.

So that was exactly what I was going to do.

Chapter Four

"Do you know Josh Johnson?" I asked Lonnie on our way to the football field the next day.

It was all part of my plan. When we'd had to choose a small scene of *Hamlet* and find a modern-day equivalent, I'd earned a few laughs by choosing Hamlet's "We'll teach you to drink deep ere you depart" scene.

I'd thought Mrs. Lynch would argue, but she just smiled and said that Hamlet's male bonding was an important part of the play.

Lonnie had raised his hand and asked to work with me, which gave me some kind of funny feeling. It was okay, though. I didn't mind having backup as I approached the football team—not that Lonnie was going to impress them, but at least I wasn't alone.

"Absolutely, I know Josh," Lonnie said as we climbed the stands beside the athletic field. "His dad is my dad's boss. And a real charmer he is, too."

When we reached a railing, I paused. I was out of breath and, I had to admit, a little out of shape.

"There he is." Lonnie leaned over my shoulder and pointed toward the football field in that too-close way he had. His body felt warm behind mine.

"Where?" I asked, as much to prolong the feeling as to get the answer.

Lonnie took my hand and pointed with it, his breath hot on my neck. "Right there," he said in a low, sexy voice.

My heart went pit-a-pat. And then I thought of Nate and felt ashamed. Here I was enjoying a silly little attraction to one boy and planning a seduction campaign on another when Nate was supposed to be my boyfriend.

But then again, Nate was hanging around Jessica and Tanika, if the ALTLIVES game was for real. I had to guess that they were flirting with him the same way I was flirting with Lonnie.

I leaned back against Lonnie, thinking. The campaign for Josh was really about my mom and getting to live with her, I reminded myself. And then Linden Falls and Linden High would be out of the picture.

And so would Lonnie. I stepped away from him. "What's Josh doing?"

Lonnie didn't answer for a minute, and I looked at him. He gave me a sexy smile. But then I noticed he was sweating, even though it was a cool fall day.

I tamped down my little adrenaline rush and turned back to the field. The good-looking guy Lonnie had identified as Josh was yelling at another kid who'd been gathering up helmets and supplies.

Lonnie cleared his throat. "He's racking someone smaller than himself, naturally."

"Racking?" You had to love those Englishisms.

"Throwing sand in the face of, figuratively. Picking on."

"Oh." I watched Josh shove the smaller kid, who looked like he was about to cry, and I didn't have to be the genius I was to know that would be a social mistake.

"I want to meet him," I said, and started down toward the field.

"You can't just walk onto the field," Lonnie argued behind me.

"Watch me." I sidled along the front row of the stands until I was standing directly over the small crowd gathered around Josh and his victim.

"What's a big boy like you doing on the sidelines?" I asked in a voice everyone could hear.

Josh stopped teasing the little guy and looked up at me. Around him, the crowd was silent. It could go either way: Josh could bully me or admire me, and of course the crowd would go the way he went.

My heart pounded in a half-pleasant, half-sick way. I leaned forward and tilted my head at him, not smiling. Girls smile too much. "Well?" I said.

"You talkin' to me?"

"You're the biggest boy out there." A little flattery never hurt.

Josh made a little half-turn away from his victim and took a step toward me. "I'm no boy."

"Oh," I said. "What, then? A girl?"

A couple people snickered.

Josh's face got a little bit redder. I could tell he wasn't used to anyone messing with him. Typical bully.

"No," he said. "Are you?"

"Well, if you have to ask . . ."

More snickers from the crowd. Behind me, I heard Lonnie draw in his breath.

This wasn't going exactly the way I'd hoped. I wanted to draw Josh away from the scared little redhead, but I didn't want him to pick on me. I wanted him to like me, to ask me to be his date for the Fall Dance, and to make me popular enough to impress my mom.

I decided to take a different approach. Leaning over the railing, I smiled at him and said, "I'm doing a project for English and I need to talk to you."

He stared straight at my chest, and not in a subtle way, either. His leering was obvious enough that a few of the other guys started laughing.

I held my position, but a slow burn started inside me. What a jerk.

Then again, maybe I'd asked for it.

"What do you guys want to talk about?" he asked, moving closer. The way he said it, it was like he was talking to my boobs, a joke the other boys also found extremely amusing.

Lonnie moved up to stand beside me. "We're doing a project analyzing male bonding, and what better place to study it than the playing field?" he asked.

I knew what Lonnie was doing: deflecting the attention from me and my chest. Just like I'd done for the little redhead, who now hovered on the edge of the crowd.

And it worked. "It's called a football field, geek," Josh said.

"Quite right. You Americans do call this little game football, don't you?"

Oh, great. Lonnie and Josh were about to get stuck in a male ego fight. It could have no good outcome for Lonnie.

"Look," I said, "I just want to do my interview for English. Can't we all just get along?"

"I can get along with you, babe," said Josh. "It's him I got the problem with."

Bingo. I was on my way.

And Lonnie would have to go. I didn't want to hurt his feelings. In fact, I wished I could just leave with him and talk about what had happened and how ridiculous Josh was.

But that wouldn't help me reach my goal. "Will you let me interview you?" I asked Josh. "He doesn't have to be there."

I didn't look at Lonnie.

"I guess, to help out a new girl, I could let you talk to me," Josh said. "Go ahead. Ask your questions."

But that wasn't what I wanted. Not only was it pretty taxing to talk to him in front of his group of admirers, but I knew I needed to get him alone.

"Your place or mine?" I said to Josh.

Beside me, I heard Lonnie snort in disgust. A couple of the other guys started making animal sounds, barking and growling.

Josh's neck turned red and his eyes got a speculative look in them. It was like he realized, *Hey, I might get some action out of this.*

"Your place sounds good," he said.

I let out my breath, relieved. I was pretty sure I could handle Josh if he came to my place, because Susan had cut back her working hours to be home when Kelly and I got home from school. She wasn't going to let anything happen.

"That's fine with me," I said. "Name the date, Mr. Football-Practice-Every-Day."

"How about Saturday?" he said.

Rats. Saturday was unpredictable; I didn't know if Susan would be around or not.

But new girls can't be choosers. I had to make this work. "Saturday afternoon's fine," I said, and blew him a kiss. "See you then."

Chapter Five

Saturday morning, the mall gleamed bright and promising, and Kelly, my unsuspecting partner in seduction, was at my side.

Complaining.

"Why do you want my advice on clothes?" she whined as Susan waved and pulled away. "I could've slept in. Besides, you're the one who's from the city and has all this so-called style."

The truth was, I needed Kelly's help to snag Josh. But I couldn't let her know that was what I wanted, or she was sure to block it. "I want to try to fit in more," I said, "and kids have been making fun of my clothes."

It was what I'd said to Susan last night at dinner, and it had resulted in Kelly's being forced to go to the mall with me. Not to mention that Susan had given each of us a hundred dollars to spend on clothes.

Kelly ought to have been grateful. I figured she wouldn't have gotten the money, except that I had pathetically few clothes and no money, and needed it, and Susan didn't want to make Kelly jealous.

But maybe the mall, and money to spend on clothes, was old news to Kelly. She already had a huge closetful of threads.

"Let's hit Whacked," I said, glad to see a familiar store.

"Um, sure," Kelly said, her voice skeptical.

So the Linden High set didn't shop at Whacked. That figured. "Where do you usually go?" I asked.

"I get most of my clothes at Smithmore's," she said.

"Then let's go there."

I heard the nerves in my voice. This was a big day. Ever since I'd met Josh and made the plan for him to come over later today, I'd been thinking.

Clearly, I'd made the initial hook with my smart mouth and my boobs. But if I wanted him to actually date me, to ask me to the Fall Dance, I had to offer more than just a fun hookup. I had to understand Josh. I had to look respectable enough that no one would look down on him for dating me. And I had to look hot enough that it would seem worth it to a lech like him.

I knew I didn't want to go all the way with him. Josh was very cute, with spiky blond hair and big muscles. He looked a lot more grown-up than your average skinny, acne-covered boy at Linden High.

But I didn't feel that special *simpatico* that I'd felt with Nate. Or that I was starting to feel with Lonnie. And if I hadn't gone all the way with Nate, there was no way I'd give it up for a small-town football bully.

No, Josh was strictly a business proposition. He had something I wanted, and in turn, I had to give him something he wanted. Or at least make him think he was going to get it.

We walked into Smithmore's junior depart-ment. I looked around. There were some cute jeans and skirts, but everything was super-expensive. My hundred dollars would be gone before I'd gotten one new look, and I knew that catching Josh would be a longer-term project.

"So who are the hot couples at school?" I asked Kelly as I held a sweater up to myself in front of a mirror.

"Why?" she asked, watching me.

I shrugged, put the sweater back, and picked up another one. "I don't know. I guess . . ." It came to me. "I'd like to date one of the football players, and I wondered what kind of girls they like."

She snorted so hard she spit out her gum. It landed right in a store mannequin's hand, and we both giggled as the saleswoman frowned our way.

Once Kelly recovered, she shook her head.

"Give up that idea. You're not a football player's type."

"What's their type?" I asked. "You?"

"Well . . . kinda," she said.

"Blond and skinny?"

"I guess." She frowned. "But I'm not a cheer-leader, and they do like those. Plus, they all have different tastes, of course."

I looked at my watch. It was almost eleven o'clock, and Josh was coming at two. Things were moving way too slow.

"What about Josh Johnson?" I blurted.

Her head snapped around. "Why?"

I shrugged. "I saw him around, that's all."

She started looking at shirts on a round rack. The plastic hangers clicked as she flipped each shirt aside. "You don't want to go out with Josh."

"Why not?" I held up another sweater and watched her in the mirror. She was frowning. "Who does he date? Did you ever go out with him?"

"Actually, I did," she said.

"So he likes girls like you, then."

"He likes *all* girls," she said, her voice bitter.

"Rich girls? Blond girls?"

She stopped clicking shirts and looked straight at me, so hard I turned around to meet her eyes.

"Mostly," she said, "Josh just likes to be first."

I felt my mouth drop open. "Was he your, I mean, did you—"

She shook her head. "No, no way. I don't do that, and everybody knows it. Which, I later figured out, is exactly why he asked me out. To see if he could change my mind. When he couldn't—" She shrugged. "Sayonara."

"Were you upset?"

"Yeah," she said, "but I'm not anymore. He's a jerk."

My mind felt like a high-speed computer, processing what Kelly said and what she didn't say, too. "So he likes virginal," I said.

"Yeah, but not too. That's what he told everyone, anyway. That I was too uptight."

"Nice," I muttered absently. I wasn't surprised he'd been a loudmouthed jerk to her; I'd already pegged him as that.

Still, for whatever reason, he was a school powerhouse. I could tell from the way Kelly talked, her elaborate calm, that she'd worked hard to seem like she didn't care. That was what you had to do when cool guys put you down.

I felt a flash of sympathy for Kelly. And a little flash of worry for myself. Even Kelly, who didn't like me, was warning me against Josh, and I was planning to walk right into his trap.

Only it wasn't his trap, I reminded myself. If everything went as planned, he'd walk into *my* trap.

And just like that, a strategy came to me. "Are

47

you done here?" I asked. "Want to go look at shoes?"

An hour later, we were in the car riding home. In my bags were the high-heeled boots and lacy new push-up bras I'd spent my money on.

I leaned forward and cleared my throat. "I really appreciate the money you gave me, Susan," I said. I wasn't lying, either. She was the first foster mother who'd given me money out of her own pocket, instead of making me wait for the clothing allowance from the state.

"It's no problem," she said. "You need some new clothes. I wish we could give you more."

"That's just it," I said. "It would cost so much to get me a whole new wardrobe, but my old clothes just don't work here. So I was wondering . . ."

"What?" Susan sounded wary, and Kelly looked interested.

"I was wondering if I could have, or borrow, some of Kelly's old clothes." I watched Kelly's mouth open to complain. "Just the old ones," I said to her quickly. "Whatever you don't wear anymore."

"I don't have any clothes I don't wear," Kelly said.

"Oh, Kelly," Susan said. "You've got at least twenty skirts and thirty sweaters. Think of the boxes downstairs we haven't even brought up for the winter. Surely some of those—"

"They wouldn't fit her," Kelly said.

I kept my smile from showing. "You wear your clothes kind of loose," I said. "I bet some of them would fit."

"Bringing up all those winter clothes and trying them on would be an excellent activity for you two," said Susan as she pulled up to the house. "I have to go to the office for the afternoon. There's sandwich stuff in the refrigerator."

"Thanks." I got out of the car, but not before I saw Susan put a restraining hand on Kelly's arm. "I mean it, Kelly," I heard her say. "This is an opportunity for you to be generous and share what you have."

She didn't add, "With those less fortunate," but she might as well have.

Well, fine. Let them use me to do their good deed for the day if it made them feel better about themselves.

I'd gotten over having low self-esteem about being poor years ago. After all, I was just a kid. It wasn't my fault that so far the adults around me hadn't had money.

Of course, if I could get back together with my mom, all of that would change.

I hustled Kelly through lunch and got all sweaty and dusty carrying up boxes of her clothes from the basement. Then I checked my watch, took a quick shower, and started trying stuff on.

Even though Kelly would only let me try about a tenth of what was in the boxes, I could tell from the mirror and the look on her face that it was working. With my new bras emphasizing my chest and the boots I'd bought playing up my legs, Kelly's sweet little skirts and sweater sets took on a whole new image.

"Skanky," she said.

"A little bit of skank can be a good thing." I reached toward the stack of sweaters.

The doorbell rang.

My heart started thumping like a drum.

Kelly looked out the window and frowned. "What's Josh Johnson doing here?"

"He's helping me with a school project," I said from inside the cutest of the sweaters.

When I popped my head out, she was staring at me with accusation all over her face. "You're trying to get Josh Johnson," she said. "And you're using my clothes to do it."

Chapter Six

"Wow, you look great," Josh said as I opened the door.

"Thanks," I said without smiling. Even though I was trying to attract him, I wasn't going to act like he was king of the universe. A lech was a lech, and that's what he looked like as he stared at my chest. "Come on in."

"Trinity," Kelly said from behind me, "I need to talk to you."

"Hey, Kelly." Josh gave her a little salute.

"Hey." She turned and walked into the kitchen, clearly expecting me to follow.

"I'll just be a minute," I told Josh, "and then we'll go upstairs."

"Upstairs sounds good to me." He was practically drooling.

"Because that's where the *computer* is," I said over my shoulder, then walked into the kitchen.

51

Kelly stood in front of the stove, hands on her hips. "You planned this all along," she said.

"Planned what?"

"To get my clothes. To invite Josh over."

I shrugged. "It's true I need clothes and can't afford them. And it's true I have to do a report for geek English on real-world male bonding, and Josh is my main source of information."

"Josh is interested in another kind of bonding," Kelly said. "Mom doesn't allow us to have boys over when she's not here."

I lifted my hands, palms up. "I didn't know."

The kitchen door opened and Josh sauntered in. "Problems, ladies?" he asked. "Can I help?"

Kelly rolled her eyes. "Trinity, you're gonna be in big trouble."

"Because of me?" Josh asked. "Aw, Kelly. You know I'm a nice guy."

"Yeah, right." She grabbed her purse and jacket off the hook by the back door and gave me a look that said, *I warned you*. "Have fun, guys."

"Kelly—"

She glanced at me, grabbed Susan's cell phone, and walked out the door, slamming it behind her.

I watched her go and my stomach did a backflip. When I'd set this up with Josh, I'd envisioned having him over with the whole family here. Now we had the house to ourselves.

And he was headed my way.

And, wow, was he big.

He put his hands on my shoulders. "Thanks for inviting me over," he said in a low voice he obviously thought was sexy. "We're gonna have a good time."

"I'm glad you're so excited about my English report," I said, twisting away. "C'mon. The computer's upstairs."

He followed me up, which made me incredibly self-conscious about the snug little skirt of Kelly's I had on.

Maybe wearing super-tight clothes wasn't such a good idea.

I tried to think, to plan. I tried to remember back to when Mom worked guys for what she could get out of them. How had she strung them along? How had she kept them from taking advantage of her? How had she kept from feeling like a shallow, manipulative wench in the process?

Or had she?

And the most pressing question: How was I going to make Josh keep his hands to himself, at least until I had him ready to ask me to the dance?

I'd had years of experience at fending off guys, between the foster homes and the schools I'd gone to. The difference was, I had to fend off Josh while keeping him interested.

I decided I had to know my opposition. And I

had to take control. "Sit down there," I ordered, pointing to a chair next to the desk.

"I'd rather sit closer to you."

"Down, boy. I'm running this show." I took the seat in front of the computer and was relieved when he plopped down in the chair I'd indicated.

"Okay." I opened up my file for English class and read through the few notes I'd taken. "Okay, male bonding in *Hamlet* compared to today. What do you talk about with your friends, Josh?"

"Girls," he said.

That figured. "What about them?"

"You sure you want to know?"

"Give me the G-rated version," I said. "And if you guys talk about anything else besides girls, tell me that, too."

"We talk about football, what happened in practice or a game, and who's getting scholarships at what college, stuff like that." He paused and it looked like he was actually thinking.

I started typing his answer into the computer and then I realized the parallels. "Hamlet and his friends talk about career ambitions, too," I said, grabbing for my Shakespeare book to find the reference.

He ignored me. "But I'd have to say a lot is about girls. How they look, you know, their bodies."

"That fits, too!" I ran my finger down the page. "Listen to this. Hamlet and his friends are joking about fortune, Lady Fortune. You know, that's like luck, like when you and your friends talk about winning or losing games."

Josh's eyes glazed over. He was obviously underwhelmed by my insights into Shakespeare.

But what else was I going to talk to him about? It wasn't as if we had anything in common.

Maybe he'd go for a bawdy joke. "Listen, you'll like this. Hamlet says, 'In the secret parts of Fortune?' And his friend says, 'Faith, her privates we.' Get it?"

"No," Josh said.

" 'Privates' is, like, the body parts of girls. Like you and your friends talk about. Only Hamlet and his friends are talking about a mythological woman, Lady Fortune." I couldn't help but get excited. I was going to get a good paper out of this.

Lonnie would love it. If it were Lonnie sitting here instead of Josh, we'd be going wild, embellishing, figuring it out, thinking of more comparisons.

But this wasn't my day for geek fun. Josh stood, and I heard his heavy tread coming toward me as I typed.

He leaned over me, his hands on either side, studying the computer screen. "I'm glad to help," he said.

He was practically nuzzling my neck. I tried to twist away, but his incredibly muscular arm blocked my escape. I kept my eyes on the computer screen, listened to Josh's heavy breathing, and just about choked on his aftershave, a musky, spicy smell. His cheek, much more stubbled than Nate's, brushed against mine.

"Josh," I said. "Take a couple steps back. You're trapping me."

I caught a glimpse of the ALTLIVES icon and tried to focus on it. If I could make this work, I could get my mom back.

Josh didn't step back as I'd asked. "I like trapping you. You feel great." His hands moved from the desk to slide down my arms.

I scooted the chair back into him, fast, and stood up and stepped away. But he was right there, jumping lightly to land in front of me.

Damn those football moves.

He wrapped his arms around me and his half-open mouth aimed itself for mine.

I turned my face away. "Stop it," I tried to yell, but my fear made my voice all breathy. Why had I brought him up here when I was in the house alone? Why hadn't I listened to Kelly and sent him home? "I said, back off. My family's gonna be back any minute."

He lifted his hands to my shoulders and leaned backward to look into my eyes. "Your family? You don't have a family."

Ooh, I did *not* like this boy.

His face was red and he was breathing hard, and perspiration glistened on his upper lip. Still, he must have read my expression. "Sorry," he said. "I didn't mean it bad. I just never knew anybody who was a foster kid before."

"I have a family." My jaw was clenched so tight it hurt.

"I'm sorry," he repeated. "I just wanna kiss you. I'm not trying to, you know, jump you."

"You could have fooled me." I twisted away from him.

"Come sit down with me," he said, taking my hand and tugging me toward the couch. "Let's just relax a minute. Okay?"

My heart rate was slowing down. I knew I wasn't attracted to Josh, but it was good to know he could see reason. He wasn't into date rape.

Everything in me wanted to send him out the door and just be by myself. But I knew if I did that, my whole plan to become Fall Queen was down the drain.

So I sat down next to him.

Wrong move. He took that as a "yes" and planted his lips on mine.

Try to relax, I told myself, and then I couldn't do it. I lifted my hands to press against his brawny chest.

The study door flew open and banged the wall behind it.

"Trinity!" It was Susan's shocked voice.

Chapter Seven

Josh let go of me and jumped up. His sweats were twisted around funny, his shirt hung out, and his guilty face brought to life the expression, "caught with his pants down."

Susan must've thought so, too. "Get out," she said to Josh.

His neck was bright red. "Sorry," he said, and took off down the stairs without a backward look at me.

"Thanks a lot," I said. I started to stand up and then, feeling shaky, sat back down. Things had been getting out of hand with Josh and I was mighty glad Susan had come home early. Kelly must have called her.

Even if she'd meant to get me in trouble, I was grateful. But no way was I going to admit that.

Kelly was actually giggling. "He was walking

so weird," she said. "Wouldn't you hate to be a boy?"

"This isn't funny, Kelly." Susan's voice was stiff and angry. "Trinity, what were you thinking, having a boy like Josh up here unsupervised?"

"I was working on getting a date to the Fall Dance," I admitted.

"You think Josh'll take you to the Fall Dance?" Kelly came all the way into the room to stare at me. "Are you crazy?"

"Why wouldn't he?" I asked. I really wanted to know.

"You're new, you're in geek classes, and you're not his type. Plus, he can get any girl in the school, including the most beautiful ones and the complete sluts. And the popular, beautiful sluts."

"Kelly! I won't have you using that word."

"At least I'm not acting like one," she said.

It took effort, but I didn't hit her. "How do you know how I'm acting?" I asked. "He was just trying to kiss me."

"With his hand up your skirt," Kelly said. "Or I should say, *my* skirt."

"Which is way too short and tight on you," Susan added.

They were double-teaming me and it wasn't fair. "Look, the skirt was working and I was getting somewhere."

"Where's your self-respect?" Susan looked

disgusted. "Using tight clothes to get a date is hardly a recipe for happiness."

I lay my head back on the couch. What world was Susan living in, anyway? Didn't she know that all girls dressed to attract boys? Hadn't she ever put on a short skirt herself, back in the day? No wonder she didn't have a man.

"And even if you let him, you know, *do* you," Kelly added in a practical tone, "that doesn't mean he'll take you to the dance. He can get all he wants without making any promises."

Susan put both hands up to the sides of her head and shook it back and forth. "You girls are fifteen! We shouldn't even be having this conversation!"

Kelly and I looked at each other. "Mom, you should know from your work that girls start having sex way younger than fifteen," she said.

"Yeah," I added. "By our age, they're into whips and chains." And then I looked at Kelly, only half joking. "You think Josh goes for bondage?"

Susan's eyes narrowed. "Okay, ladies, listen up." Her voice was beyond lawyer and well into judge. She held up a finger. "Number one, the rule is that you can't have boys here when I'm not home, and you can *never* have them upstairs. Understand?"

I nodded.

She looked at Kelly.

"I know, I know! I'm not the one who—"

"It's worth a review." She held up another finger. "Number two, I think both of you could benefit from giving some thought to your values. So . . ." She tapped her chin, thinking.

Oh, no. It was going to be a Susan punishment. Didn't she ever just haul off and smack her kid?

She raised her eyebrows and smiled. "I know what. At church tomorrow, we're going to find a service activity we can all do together."

"Gee, that sounds really fun," I said.

Kelly said, "I thought taking *her* in was enough service for anyone!"

Ouch.

"Kelly, come downstairs with me. Trinity, we're not through talking about all of this." Susan, like an angry superhero, ushered Kelly out of the room at the same time she gave me the evil eye.

After they left, I sat down at the computer—technically still off limits—and punched up ALT-LIVES.com. I wanted to see what my real mom was doing. And I wanted to escape from Susan, Josh, and Linden Falls.

Maybe I'd been wrong about my plan. Maybe becoming queen of the Fall Dance wasn't the right way to go about impressing her. Or maybe there was another way to do it besides Josh. I really didn't want to spend the next few weeks, plus the dance night itself, fending him off.

If I had a little more time, I could think of a

Plan B. A way to get Mom's attention that didn't make me feel small and dirty inside.

I'd spent the past couple of days using the school computers to check out what I'd learned on ALTLIVES, and as far as I could tell, it was accurate. What Mom had said matched the online archives of the *Post-Gazette's* "Seen" column. I'd even found her new married name listed, along with her husband's, at several events. Hector and June Alvarez.

Unfortunately my caseworker was on an extended vacation and no one at the agency seemed to know when, or if, he was going to be back. So I couldn't question him about the site and how and why it worked.

I WANT TO SEE MY MOM, I typed.

She is currently unavailable flashed back at me.

Oh, yeah? Up to now, I'd always gotten to see or hear her when I'd asked.

HOW COME? I typed.

She is not fully clothed.

That made my face feel hot. I checked the time. What was my mom doing undressed at 3:15 on a Saturday afternoon? WHAT'S SHE DOING? I typed, then wished I hadn't asked.

She is dressing after a doctor's appointment.

Uh-oh. CAN I SEE HER WHEN SHE'S DRESSED?

Instead of words, the screen flashed with that now-familiar low-quality video image. My mom came through a door into a room and sat down next to a rich, well-dressed man in front of a desk. Behind the desk was a doctor.

She didn't look sick. But she looked worried. And I suddenly realized I needed to hear the words more than I needed to see the players.

I NEED TO SWITCH TO AUDIO, I typed.

Immediately, the video switched off and I heard voices. This was the first time I'd heard Mom's voice, and it choked me up. So much so that at first I didn't get the gist of what she was saying.

"I'm too young to have fertility problems," she said.

"Is it me, Doctor?" asked a man's deep voice. This must be her husband, Hector. "Because June isn't even thirty yet."

Had I heard that right? Mom was well over thirty, at least thirty-three.

But apparently, her rich, smart husband didn't know it.

"It's been more than a year," she was saying, "and we haven't conceived yet. We don't want to wait any longer to start our family."

Whoa! *Start* your family? Honey, your family was started fifteen years ago, and you haven't done such a spectacular job of . . .

Wait a minute. What exactly was going on here?

I half listened while the doctor droned on about fallopian tubes and varicoceles and gross things that could be done with a needle and a petri dish.

My mind raced. If Mom was trying to have another baby, then she must want to be a mom. Maybe she didn't know where I was.

Or maybe she wanted a *new* baby, a little tiny baby. Just like most people.

Rather than a teenager who dressed and acted like a slut.

The whole inside of my chest and stomach ached. I tuned back into the words coming out of the computer speakers. "Maybe you'd like to go home and think and talk about all of this," the doctor said. He had one of those soothing doctor voices.

"We already know we want to start right away," the man, Mom's husband, said.

"Yes, oh yes," Mom said. But there was something wrong. She was being fake. "Except . . . there is our cruise, dear. Maybe we should wait until that's past. If I'm right in thinking we need to be in town and available for the treatments?"

"If you want to move forward aggressively, I'd recommend that you cancel vacation plans, or wait to start treatment until afterwards," the doctor said. "Not only because your trip could fall at the time we need to do an ultrasound or a special injection, but because air travel affects fertility."

"Oh—"

"We can cancel the cruise," her husband said, his voice decisive. "It's just the Caribbean. Nothing special. I would rather not wait two months to begin."

Mom was quiet for a second too long before she said, "Of course."

I knew exactly what was going through her head, and if her husband didn't, he was a piss-poor reader of people. No way did she want to cancel their cruise. The Caribbean might be old news to him, but to Mom it was a lifetime dream.

Having kids wasn't. She already knew she didn't like it much.

If I could do the Fall Queen thing in a way that impressed him, too, maybe I'd be enough daughter for both of them. They could go ahead and do their cruise, *and* have a great child to be proud of. Heck, they could take their child on the cruise with them!

All I had to do was to figure out what would impress him as well as her.

And I had to do it fast.

Chapter Eight

"Let me use the cell phone," I ordered Kelly Saturday night.

"Why?"

"I'm depressed, and I want to call Nate."

We were at the grocery store instead of the movie we'd planned to see. Susan had decided we needed more responsibilities and more to think about besides boys, and she'd dropped us off with instructions to buy only what was on the list, the cheapest version that looked half decent, and to call her with any questions.

Actually, I think she just wanted a break from us and from grocery shopping.

Nate hadn't been returning my e-mails, which gave me a sick, scared feeling. But after my icky encounter with Josh, I needed to talk to someone who cared about me.

And maybe there was nothing wrong between

me and Nate. Maybe he just hadn't gotten to a computer lately. He was pretty busy. Which was why I wanted to call.

Kelly, however, wasn't cooperating. "Mom doesn't allow us to use it except to call her," she said in her good-girl voice. "It's too expensive."

"Come on, she won't care," I said.

"No way." Kelly tucked her purse, which held the cell phone, more tightly over her shoulder. "Anyway, we've got to shop. It's your fault we're here instead of at the movies. If you hadn't gotten all passionate with Josh—"

"I know, I know." We were wandering aimlessly, our cart almost empty, because neither of us knew squat about groceries.

"Omigod, look." We'd just turned a corner and there was a girl, Tracey, from our school. In the diaper aisle. With a baby on her hip.

"Now there's the kind of girl Josh likes to use and throw away," Kelly said. "She's a real tramp. But I didn't know she had . . . omigod, wait 'til I tell the girls."

I frowned. Tracey was actually in my honors English class and was the only half-cool girl there, except for her unfortunate liking for fishnet stockings. We'd spoken a few times and she was someone I thought I could be friends with . . . if I was staying in Linden Falls, which I definitely wasn't.

"I didn't know she had a baby," I said as we moved closer.

"Me either. This is so weird."

Just then Tracey turned and saw us. "Hey," she said without interest, and went back to studying the diapers.

"Hi, Tracey," Kelly said in an overly friendly way. "Aw, he's so cute! What's his name?"

"Susie," she said. "She's a girl."

"Is she yours?" I asked, causing Kelly to poke me in the side. Obviously, she didn't think I should ask something like that, but I was curious how Tracey could've hidden something like a baby in Linden Falls.

"No. My sister's." She shifted the baby into her other arm. "She dumped him on me to babysit without any diapers. These suckers are expensive."

"Try these." I pointed to a package of the brand I'd seen most often in foster homes. It had to be the cheapest.

She checked out the price. "Hey, thanks."

"See you in class." I pushed the cart on.

Kelly was still looking back at Tracey. "Man, that shocked me. I thought that baby was hers."

"It happens," I said. Then I snaked my hand over, reached into her purse, and grabbed the cell phone. All without her noticing. It was nice to know I hadn't lost my touch. "Look, can you get started while I hit the bathroom? I'll catch up with you."

I left before she could say no, ran into the bathroom, and punched in Nate's number.

His mother answered. "Hello, Trinity," she said without a lot of enthusiasm. She'd never liked me. "No, Nate's not here. He's out."

"Will you ask him to call me?" I perched on the edge of the toilet, picturing Nate's handsome face.

There was a pause. Then she said, "He's pretty busy with Tanika these days. They see each other almost every day."

Her words hit me like a punch in the stomach. Could they be true?

A sinking feeling in my gut said yes. Nate hadn't stayed in touch as he'd promised. I'd seen him with the twins on ALTLIVES. And even though Nate's mom didn't like me, she wasn't the type who would lie.

If Nate had gone so far as to choose a twin, it was serious. So serious that I couldn't call him my boyfriend anymore.

All this time, through all these crazy plans about Josh, I'd felt okay because my real life was back in the city with Nate. I squeezed my eyes shut to keep from crying. All of a sudden I felt like I had no safety net, like I was totally alone in the world. "Thanks," I mumbled, and turned off the phone.

* * *

The next day, Susan, Kelly and I stood in the hallway of the Methodist church looking at the bulletin board. Or rather, Susan was looking at it. Kelly and I were complaining.

"I'm so busy with school," Kelly said. "I don't have time to do some big project for poor people or whatever."

"Yeah, and I'm poor myself. For me to help the poor is like the blind leading the blind." I waited for a laugh, but I didn't get one.

"Some people from disadvantaged backgrounds actually want to do something to help others," Susan said, continuing to study the board.

I made a face behind her back as I inhaled the musty old-building smell and toed a worn-out patch in the carpet. In some other part of the building, I could hear an organ playing and people singing.

"We could help with the rummage sale," Susan said. "Sort clothes, arrange by size, serve customers on the day of the sale. That would fit with your interest in clothes."

"Yeah," said Kelly, "maybe we could find something decent for Trinity to wear."

"Shut up," I said. I also called her a name that shouldn't be heard in the halls of a church, but I was disgusted at the idea of getting clothes at a church sale. I had some experience with that and I didn't want to repeat it.

I was so preoccupied, though, that I didn't put

any energy into fighting with Kelly, nor into the lecture from Susan that followed my cursing.

I was still reeling from what I'd discovered about Nate. I'd thought of him as my boyfriend for a whole year. It hurt to realize that wasn't going to be true anymore.

And every time I pushed Nate out of my mind, my mom popped in. I kept reviewing my ALT-LIVES encounter over and over in my mind.

If Mom was seriously going to try to have another baby, then my file was deleted. No way would she take me on when she could choose a cute new baby instead.

Not to mention that her husband would have zilch interest in having me around if he had a child of his own loins, so to speak.

But I wasn't convinced Mom wanted to have another baby. If I played the game right, I could be a substitute. I had to really impress them. I had to be the best thing that had ever happened to them.

Trouble was, just showing up at their house and announcing I'd been crowned queen of the Fall Dance didn't sound quite dramatic enough.

"Look," Kelly said finally, "couldn't we volunteer to reorganize the Fall Dance as our service project? That way it would at least be something we're interested in."

I was impressed. "That'd be cool."

"I'm not sure that would address the values problem," Susan said. "You girls are too obsessed with boys and clothes. And what's the Fall Dance about?"

"Boys and clothes," Kelly and I said together. We looked at each other and grinned.

"But the dance is falling apart because the planning committee is fighting," Kelly said. "If we could fix it, maybe we'd learn something about working with other people." She glanced at Susan, obviously wondering if she would buy this line of reasoning. "It would build our leadership skills."

Not bad. Kelly had years of experience with her mom. She knew what worked.

Susan cocked her head to one side, interested against her will.

I had to do my part. What had Susan said before? Some people from disadvantaged backgrounds actually want to help others. I let my eyes skim the bulletin board, speed-reading the various service projects, and then the perfect idea popped into my head. "We could raise money with the dance and donate it to Saint Helen's Home for Girls." I made my expression just a little bit pathetic. "It'd be helping girls like me. I could get into that."

Kelly could tell I was faking, and started to giggle, but she managed to turn the sound into a cough. I almost started laughing too, so I waved paper in Susan's face to distract her.

"Hmmm," Susan said. "I might buy into this—"

"Yes!" Kelly gave me a high five.

"If you'll find a way to get personally involved with the girls you're helping."

"You mean go to Saint Helen's?" I wasn't sure I was ready for that. "And work directly with the girls there?"

"Exactly," Susan said. "Still interested?"

"Um, I guess." I thought about going back there to help in some way. I guessed I wouldn't mind seeing my old neighborhood. "Sure."

"The other condition is that you have to raise significant funds, at least two thousand dollars, with the dance."

"Oh, man!" I looked at Kelly. Two thousand dollars was more money than I'd ever seen, and I had no idea how to go about raising it.

"We can do that," she said with complete confidence.

"Well, just to make sure," Susan said, giving us the evil eye, "I think I'll volunteer to be one of the parents who helps with the dance. I'm sure there's a need, both in the planning stages and on the actual night."

"Great, Mom," Kelly said, right on the edge of sarcasm.

"Yeah, great," I echoed. But I didn't really care. This way, we could concentrate on the dance instead of some dumb rummage sale. I'd get to see my old neighborhood. And most importantly, I could stay focused on my goal.

* * *

It was later that night, while indulging my addiction to spying on my mom, that I got my big idea.

Just like before, she was talking to her maid about the "Seen" section of the paper. Once again, she'd been left out of the pictures at some benefit ball she had attended.

"How much money do you have to give to get in the papers?" she asked, obviously without expecting an answer. "We paid a thousand dollars per plate, but that's not enough?"

Maybe it was the number she named, a thousand dollars—half the amount Susan had said we had to raise. Maybe it was the mention of a benefit ball.

What if we made her and her husband the headline, keynote, big-deal sponsors of our dance? And promised them press coverage?

They'd have to come, of course. That would mean they would be there for my triumph as Queen of the Fall Dance.

Mom would get her picture in the paper . . . at least, if I, or Susan, could talk the newspaper into coming. It might not be the big-city paper Mom wanted, but in the *Cow Land Weekly,* it would make the front page.

All I had to do was find out from Susan how a benefit ball would work, and convince her I knew someone who could donate the big bucks.

And then call my mom and get her to agree.

Chapter Nine

"So does anyone have a dress for the Fall Dance yet?" asked Stephanie, Kelly's snottiest friend.

Five of us had crowded into a booth at Tommy's Pizzeria. Kelly, three of her very closest friends, and me. Not that anyone wanted me here, and not that I really wanted to be here, but I'd forced Kelly to bring me.

I wasn't going to get Josh to ask me to the Fall Dance by sitting at home. I'd heard he and his friends usually hung out here, so when Kelly announced she was going, I asked if she'd take me. In Susan's hearing, which meant Kelly couldn't say no.

"Not only do I not have a dress, I don't have a date, either," Kelly admitted. It was one thing I admired about her: she was honest and didn't put up a front.

"Me either," said Joan. Her chunky build and

acne made her the least attractive of Kelly's friends.

"Oh, you guys will get asked," Stephanie said with the patronizing tone of a girl with a steady boyfriend. "Travis hasn't bought our tickets yet himself."

"He'd better hurry up," Kelly said. "The last day to buy tickets is Friday."

"Yeah, what's up with that?" asked another girl whose name I kept forgetting. "Why the deadline?"

"Some kind of security thing," Kelly said. "Now that Mom's on the planning committee with us, she's bringing up all the legal issues."

Our pizza came, hot and greasy, along with a bunch of plates. All the girls acted like they didn't want to dig in, but I wasn't into waiting and I certainly wasn't dieting. I grabbed a piece and started eating.

Joan followed suit, and then so did the rest of the girls, except Stephanie. "I can't," she explained. "I'm really trying to stay a size six."

She gave me and Joan a raised-eyebrow look. I rolled my eyes. Joan looked devastated.

"People like the way that looks around here, do they?" I asked.

"The way what looks?" Stephanie snapped.

I took another slice of pizza and made sure to wave it under her nose. "The bony look," I said.

She flushed and didn't say anything for a

minute, but the blessed silence couldn't last, of course.

"How'd you get on the dance committee, anyway?" asked the other girl, whose name, I now remembered, was Trish. "It's not like you know much about how things work around here."

"Mom made us do a service activity so we'd get, quote, better values," Kelly explained.

"Some people could use some," Stephanie said, looking at me.

"You're one to talk," I retorted.

Stephanie ignored me. "So what's this I hear about how you're not supposed to rent limos or wear corsages for this dance? Whose big idea was that? Hers?" She sneered in my direction.

"It's to save money you can donate to Saint Helen's Home for Girls," Kelly explained. "I know, it sucks not to wear a corsage, but it's a good cause."

"I'm not doing it," Stephanie said. "I mean, I'll make the donation, but I'll also make Travis buy me a corsage."

"Nope," I said with pleasure. "You won't be allowed in with one."

"That is so ridiculous!" Stephanie fumed. "Like I really care about some Home for Girls! And now you're ruining my dance—"

"Spare me." I made a gagging sound.

Kelly gave me a look that said "shut up" plain

as day. All the girls tended to cater to Stephanie's mood.

Not me. I made like I was playing the violin. "Poor little Stephanie. Doesn't get to wear a corsage. Never mind that other teenagers don't have a home or a family: Steph needs her flowers!"

"Shut up!" she screamed. "Who asked you to come here and ruin everything?"

I grinned. Finally, someone with some fighting energy in Podunk. "Thanks for giving me the power to ruin your life," I said.

Around us, the restaurant had gotten a little quiet and people were staring. I wiped the grease off my hands and grabbed my soda, because I had a feeling I wouldn't be at the table much longer.

Especially if I ended up throwing it at Stephanie.

The door of the place opened with a jingle. Josh Johnson strode in with his friends behind him.

Immediately, the atmosphere at my table changed. A catfight no longer compelled us. Instead, there was a lot of mouth-wiping and hair-combing and lipstick reapplication.

Josh headed for a table across the room, near the TV and a couple of video games. He pretended not to see us, but the way he swaggered could only have been for our benefit. His friends, naturally, followed his lead.

"I wonder who Josh is taking to the dance," Trish said.

Kelly threw a glance at me. "One thing's for

sure, he'll wait until the last minute. He likes to keep all his hopefuls on a string."

"He's so cute," Joan said.

This was getting me nowhere. "Think I'll play some Pod," I said, and got up and away from the table before any of them could comment.

Pod was the video game right next to Josh's table. It was a bold move, going over there alone when there were at least five of Josh's cronies over there. Most girls wouldn't have done it, wouldn't have had the nerve.

But I wasn't most girls.

Plus I was desperate. So I walked over with my best swing, bent over, and fed money into the machine.

The effect would've been better if I'd been wearing one of Kelly's tight skirt-and-sweater outfits. But Susan had nixed that whole wardrobe improvement and bought me a couple new pairs of jeans. I was wearing the tighter ones with a zip-up hoodie.

Considerably unzipped, of course.

Pretending I didn't see the boys, I started playing the game. It was actually a medieval-style thing with a girl lead character, interesting enough that I could focus on it and not on them.

A little while later, I felt a hand on my back.

Josh.

I half-turned without letting go of the game controls. "Hey," I said.

He leaned closer. "I didn't expect to see you here."

"I get around," I said, and dodged an arrow someone shot at my game character.

"Thought you might be grounded," he boomed out.

I frowned and looked at him. "Why?"

"Because of Saturday." He was saying all this very loudly, which confused me until I realized he was trying to impress his homies. What had he told them about Saturday? Surely he hadn't bragged that he'd kissed me, gotten a little too excited, and gotten caught?

No, of course not. He must have said, or implied, that he'd gotten some real action at my house.

My mind raced with how to play it. If I called him on his exaggeration he'd look bad in front of his friends, which I already knew he hated. But if I acted like we'd actually done the nasty, the whole school would think I was a complete slut.

Either way, I wouldn't rate high enough to be his date at the Fall Dance.

I turned around suddenly to face him, my back against the machine. In the video game, I heard my character die.

"No, I didn't get grounded," I said. "I was more worried about you. Was it hard walking home?" I placed just the teeniest extra emphasis on the word *hard*.

Josh had opened his mouth to speak. He took a breath in, and shut it.

His friends broke out laughing.

I held his eyes and let a little smile cross my face.

A flush crept up his neck and onto his cheeks. Finally, he grinned. "Yeah, it was hard," he said.

"Thought so." I turned back to the game, but not before I saw Kelly and Trish approaching. Back at the girls' table, Joan seemed to be trying to get Stephanie to come along.

"Hi, Josh," Trish said in that offhand flirty way I use myself. Then she and Kelly leaned over the video game and acted all interested in it.

"My character died," I told them. "Anyone got money?"

That led to a lot of pocket-hunting and hair-tossing and sauntering walks back to the table. Kelly did the smart thing and asked the guys from Josh's table if she could borrow a buck.

Of course they all fell over themselves to give it to her. She was really cute and nice. She'd have a date for the Fall Dance in a minute if she would just act a little bit available. Most guys probably thought she was taken.

I felt lucky she wasn't after Josh.

Speaking of him, he'd stepped away from me when all the other girls came over. I guess he didn't want to ruin his chances with them by appearing to show a preference for me.

The rat. Now he was sitting at the table.

And Trish was about to move in.

I couldn't let that happen. I came up behind Josh and leaned forward, putting my cheek next to his. My breasts nuzzled his back.

"Hey," I whispered.

He leaned backward with that dazed look a breast guy gets in the vicinity of two sizable mamas. "Yeah?"

"Thanks for helping with my research," I whispered right into his ear.

"Sure," he said.

"I got an 'A' on the paper."

"Great." Obviously, he was unable to put together a whole sentence.

Good. I'd distracted him from Trish.

Now, I needed to make progress toward my goal. From what the girls had said, I couldn't expect him to actually ask me to the Fall Dance tonight. But I had to be at the forefront of his mind from now until Friday, when the ticket deadline passed.

How to do it? I shouldn't have said I was done with the paper. I couldn't exactly ask him to help me with my homework.

The other guys at the table were talking and laughing about something, and now Trish and Kelly joined in.

"No way would I go to that party," Trish said.

"Me either. And even if I would, my mom wouldn't let me," said Kelly.

"What party are they talking about?" I asked Josh.

"Hey, ask Trinity!" one of the guys said. "She'll come."

"To what?" I asked. I stood up to give Josh room to breathe.

His ability to speak returned. "The football team's Thursday night bash," he said. "We always have one when there's a week off from Friday night games. It's kinda crazy, but fun." He turned around and tried to look up at my face, but his eyes just couldn't get past my chest. "Want to come?"

"Maybe," I said, stalling. "Tell me more."

"Oh, Trinity, Mom will never let you go," Kelly said. "It's just a bunch of guys out in the woods. Drinking and who knows what else."

It didn't sound so great. And yet, what other chance did I have? I wouldn't see Josh all week, since we took different classes and he always had practice. Meanwhile, tons of other girls would be working on him.

"Do other girls go?" I asked.

"Oh, yeah," said one of the guys. "Really nice ones."

"The dregs," Trish added. "You'd fit right in."

"That's not true," Josh said quickly. "There are a lot of girls there, regular girls. Kelly even came once."

I shot a glance at my foster sister. A blush stained her cheeks pink. "I came, but I left pretty

85

fast," she said. "And I told Mom about it. So you'll never be allowed."

I eyed Kelly. She didn't know how lucky she was to have a mom she could tell things to. A mom who looked out for her and tried to protect her.

She was lucky; I wasn't. Not yet.

But if I worked it right, I'd use this connection with Josh to get my real mom back.

Then I'd be lucky, too.

I smiled down at Josh, trying to put promises in my eyes. Promises I didn't intend to keep. "Sure," I told him. "I'll go."

Chapter Ten

"Rumor has it you're partying with the football team this week," said a British-accented voice beside me.

I'd thought this corner of the school library was private. I'd come here, skipping lunch, because I didn't feel like being with people. Apparently, Josh and his friends had spread the word that I was coming to the Thursday night bash.

Lonnie settled at the computer next to me and logged on. "So is it true?" he asked.

"What?" I studied the ALTLIVES screen.

I was playing the game out of anxiety. I dreaded the party, and wondered if it would even make a difference. Would I really be able to snag Josh for the Fall Dance? Would being Fall Queen really be enough to make Mom want me back?

And was it worth it, considering what I might have to do to get Josh to invite me?

I'd fallen into the pattern of checking the video first, to get an idea of where Mom was and what she was doing, and then switching to the transcript. Now I caught a glimpse of her all dressed up at a fancy luncheon. She was sitting next to her hubby at a big round table. She kept half-standing and looking around, as if searching for someone. Who?

I clicked the necessary keys to switch to the transcript.

"You're avoiding the question," Lonnie said.

"What was it?" I'd genuinely forgotten, and now I smiled over at him apologetically.

"Are you really going to the football bash, and have you lost your mind?"

I didn't see the point of lying. "Yes, I'm going. What's the big deal?"

"You probably ought to ask some of the girls who've been."

"So why do you care?" I challenged him.

"Because, my dear, I want you for my own. And after Josh's party, you'll be . . . taken. In more ways than one."

Only Lonnie would say it like that. "You're weird," I said.

"I care," he corrected. "You're making a mistake."

Part of me knew he was right. But I didn't want to think about it. Fortunately, the transcript came up and distracted me.

A woman with long brunette hair, dressed in a red sheath, stands at her dinner table, looking around. She appears to be oblivious to the curious stares of those around her, or the efforts of her dinner partner to make her sit down.

Finally the man succeeds in pulling her into her seat. She turns to him. "I just want to see where the photographer is. I want to show off my dress."

He laughs. "They're not going to photograph you. We paid our five hundred dollars per plate, but that's all. Didn't you ever notice that it's the big donors who get the publicity?"

"Well, why don't you give more money?" she asks.

Even I had to smile at that one. Mom has always been a little, how can I say it, simpleminded. She's not dumb, exactly, more like super-focused. She knows what she wants and she goes after it, and she doesn't really think about the side issues.

That's one way we're alike.

I wondered what her husband would say. Ignoring Lonnie, who remained at the computer next to me looking something up on the Internet, I went back to the transcript and read fast to catch up.

"I don't want to give away all our money, sweetheart," says the man. *"We'll need it for the little one."*
  "There IS no little one."
  "There could be."

Oh, Lord. I wanted so much to see their faces as they talked. I tried to get the machine to switch back to video, but in my stress I couldn't figure out how to do it.

When I cursed under my breath, Lonnie leaned over. "You could catch major trouble for playing games in the library, sweets," he said.

"Yeah, especially stupid games that drive me crazy." I studied the screen glumly. There was no more transcript, and I didn't know if they'd stopped talking or if I'd just lost contact.

"There are real-world ways to get driven crazy," Lonnie said, unexpectedly close to my ear.

His breath was warm on my neck and my heart started beating extra hard. There was something about Lonnie. Unlike most high school boys, he said what he thought, even if what he thought was that he liked you. He wasn't crude and grabby like Josh, but he was definitely sexy. I reached back to touch his arm, then, surprised, let my fingers spread out. "Where'd you get the biceps?" I asked. "Are you a gym rat?"

"Club soccer player," he growled, still next to my ear. "I'd like to see *you* in a red sheath dress."

"You were reading over my shoulder!" I spun to look at him.

"Guilty," he said, smiling and holding my eyes. "I'm a bit . . . fixated on you, Miss Trinity."

My face felt hot, and I couldn't stop looking at him. I was almost glad when the librarian came over and shooed us off the computers.

"Do you have a red dress?" Lonnie asked as we walked out into the hallway, crowded with noisy kids changing classes.

"No." I was trying not to notice how close Lonnie walked beside me.

He put a hand on my back, very gently, to guide me past a crowd of jostling boys. "What are you wearing to the Fall Dance?" he asked in my ear. "You're going, aren't you?"

"Yeah . . . I think so."

His hand felt so good on my back. It seemed to warm my whole insides.

What if Lonnie asked me to the dance? What would I say?

Should I follow my goals or my glands?

I caught a glimpse of the girls' bathroom and stopped. "I have to go in here."

"Don't run away," Lonnie said. "Come here." He pulled me over to a little nook beside the janitor's closet. It wasn't exactly private, but it was as close to it as we'd get at Linden High. I stood against the wall, and there was nowhere to look but into Lonnie's eyes.

"What did you mean, you think you're going to the Fall Dance?" he asked. He put his hands against the wall on either side of my head and leaned a little toward me. "Did someone ask you?"

"No, not yet," I said. It was hard to breathe. There was always a faint, spicy smell that came from Lonnie, some kind of cologne or soap. It made me want to kiss him.

"But you think someone's going to."

I swallowed and tried to look away. "Yeah."

"Josh?"

"How'd you know?"

He looked off to the side and took a deep breath. A vein stood out in his neck, pulsing, and I realized he was mad.

Was he jealous? And why did that thrill me so much?

I felt flushed over my entire body, and certain key parts tingled madly. I couldn't stop looking at Lonnie's lips.

This wasn't good.

"Trinity," he said finally, taking a step back and crossing his arms, "you're a very smart girl. That's just one of the things about you that turns me on."

"What are the others?" I asked, cocking my head to one side.

"Don't flirt. There's time for that later if you manage to get your act together."

"What's that supposed to mean?" I put my hands on my hips. "My act's just fine."

"Your act will get you into trouble if you go to that party chasing Josh Johnson. I'm serious, babe. He is very bad news."

I stuck out my lower lip. "You don't understand. I have my reasons for what I'm doing."

"What? Do you want him that badly?" All of a sudden Lonnie stepped forward, cupped my head in his hands, and shifted his weight so that he was almost, but not quite, touching ninety-five percent of the front of my body. "I'm no jock, but I know how to please a lady. I can make you feel good."

Oh, man. My insides burned. The temperature in the little alcove had risen about two hundred degrees. When Lonnie rubbed his thumb along my cheek, it felt like it left a trail of fire.

How did he *do* that?

He took a step backward. "I want you. And I'm your friend, too. But I won't wait forever."

He turned and walked away, leaving me to stumble blindly into the bathroom.

Once inside, I stepped into a stall, shut the door, and leaned against it, breathing hard, trying to calm down. Slowly my body came back to normal.

Lonnie made it sound like he really wanted to be my boyfriend. He was offering heart and soul, as well as some good love. What was more, he really knew me. He liked me for who I was, rather than just for my chest like some guys. Like Josh.

It was so magnetic, so appealing, so much what I wanted in the deepest part of myself.

There was only one thing I wanted more: Mom.

Stay focused, stay focused, I reminded myself. Being Lonnie's girlfriend, going to the Fall Dance with him, was not on the list of things that would impress my mom. He was smart and sexy, sure. But he was also non-athletic and stick-thin, and an outsider just like me. No way was he going to get anywhere near the awards stage.

And that meant his date wouldn't, either.

It would have been fun to date Lonnie, and I felt hot and excited inside that he liked me. But, I reminded myself, fun and excitement could come later, after I'd reached my goals. What I felt about Lonnie was just a silly attraction. What I needed from my mom would happen only if I could get crowned Fall Queen.

Thinking about the awards stage made everything clear.

My eyes went blurry as I thought about Mom and me up there on the stage, me because I was Fall Queen, her because she was the major donor for the dance.

All I had to do was get her phone number and call her.

It took me two whole days to get up the nerve.

"Mrs. Alvarez, please." My hands were totally sweating and my voice felt shaky. I huddled in my bedroom with Susan's cell phone pressed to my ear. Lonnie, showing that he meant it about being my friend, had helped me hack into a directory of unlisted numbers.

"May I ask who is calling?" Mom's maid answered the phone; I recognized her voice from ALTLIVES.

Obviously I couldn't use my own name. But I was ready with my lie. "This is Kelly Turner from Linden High School, and I'm calling with a major sponsorship opportunity."

"One moment, please."

Breathe, breathe.

"Hello?"

It was my mom's voice. For the first time since

I was eight years old, I had the chance to talk to her directly. Tears rose to my eyes and I felt like I was about to pass out.

"Hello?" She sounded impatient now.

I took a huge breath and looked down at the script I'd written. "Hello, Mrs. Alvarez. This is, um, Kelly Turner from Linden High School and I'm calling with a major sponsorship opportunity."

"I thought I told you to screen out telemarketers," she hissed. It must have been to her maid because I could barely hear it.

"I'm not a telemarketer," I said quickly. "I'm calling you, just you."

"Do I know you from somewhere?" she asked. "Your voice sounds familiar."

I had a hard time catching my breath, and my throat seemed to close. Inside of me, so many words fought to get out.

Yes, you know me; I'm the daughter you gave away!

Please, please, please take me back to live with you!

Can't you even try to be nice? I'm your daughter!

And most of all: *Mommy! Mommy, help me!*

What stopped my throat was my fear that if I identified myself directly, I'd get directly rejected. After all, it had happened before: I'd begged her to keep me, and she'd sent me away.

No, I had to go through with my plan, had to show Mom what a great kid I was, before she'd want me back. And that meant, for now, that I had to keep my identity a secret. I just had to hook her as the major sponsor of our dance and get her to come, and then everything else would fall into place—or at least I hoped it would.

I cleared my throat and sat up straight and went into the biggest acting routine in my life.

"You don't know me. I read about you and your husband in the 'Seen' column of the *Post-Gazette.*"

"Oh, really?" Interest and warmth livened her voice. "Which issue?"

"It was several months back," I said. "Mrs. Alvarez, we're a small high school with a big project." Now I was getting back to my prepared script. "We want to raise money and awareness for a center for teens in trouble." I didn't add the foster care part, figuring that she might not want to be associated with such a cause. Knowing Mom, she'd conveniently forgotten to mention to all her uptown friends that her daughter was in the foster care system.

"I don't think—"

I rushed on, pretending not to hear her protest. "We're looking for one major donor we can feature in all our publicity materials. And we're hoping to get press coverage for the Fall

Dance. We really want to raise awareness for our cause, so we're totally focusing on publicity. If you agree to be the donor, we hope you'll come." I paused, then added, "So we can honor you."

There was a silence on the other end of the phone, and something told me to let it happen. I knew Mom well enough to know I'd pushed the right buttons. Now I had to let her decide for herself.

I poured all my positive energy and prayers into the phone wires between us. I tried to project to her the sense that this was an important moment in her life, the chance to be on center stage. What she didn't yet know was that this could be her start on the road to getting her daughter back, to having the happy family that was meant to be all along.

She didn't have to have a new baby. All she had to do was to get back together with me.

I hung there, waiting.

"All right," she said finally. "I'll have to consult with my husband, of course, but if you send me the information, I think we can be your major sponsor."

All my breath came out in a huge sigh, making me dizzy.

It had worked!

My mother was coming to the dance.

And that meant I absolutely had to get Josh

Johnson to invite me there, so that I could impress Mom as the Fall Queen.

Which meant I had to play tomorrow night's party just right.

Chapter Eleven

The bonfire, the woods, and the crowd of laughing guys might have been fun if I hadn't been so afraid of what would happen later.

"Have another beer, Trinity." Josh's words sounded more like an order.

"I'm still working on this one, thanks," I said. I wished I was back at Susan's house, wearing sweats, watching a movie, and eating popcorn. That's what Kelly and Susan were doing.

Kelly was sworn to secrecy, and Susan thought I was at Tracey's house working on an honors English project. She'd been happy I was making friends on my own, which just made me feel even guiltier for lying.

It also meant there was no one to save me if I got in trouble.

I looked around at the crowd of ten drunk

boys—I was the only girl—and thought, *what am I doing here?*

It's for Mom, I reminded myself. *It's to get the date to get voted queen to get back together with Mom.*

One thing was for sure: I wasn't drinking much of this beer. For one thing, I didn't like its sharp, tongue-curling taste. For another, I didn't intend to lose any of my wits or ability to make my own choices.

"Drink up!" Josh urged. "I thought you were a party girl."

"Don't be narrow-minded," I said to him. "There are all kinds of ways to party."

His buddies laughed like I'd said something funny.

A car without a muffler slowed, then stopped nearby. Headlights swept across the clearing.

"Is it cops?" one of the younger guys asked. His buddy didn't wait to find out, but ran for the woods.

"Nah, that's Tracey's car," Josh said.

Sure enough, I heard girls' voices. That was a relief.

Tracey and two girls I didn't know came down the path and into the light of the bonfire.

I gave a little wave, one girl to another, but inside I was worrying. If those were the kind of girls who came to these events, then being here wasn't the best route to the Fall Dance. I wasn't from around here, but I assumed things were the same as in my old school: the jocks didn't date the trashy girls, though they might go off into the alley with them—or in Podunk, off into the bushes with them—at a party.

No, the jocks got their testosterone levels back down to normal at parties like this, and then asked the "nice" girls to the school dances.

But what choice did I have? I wasn't going to get invited to the nice-girl parties of jocks and cheerleaders. I could hardly go crash their table at lunch.

"Hey, Trinity," Josh said. He sounded like he had a mouth full of cotton. "Wanna go t'my car?"

There was a little silence, like everyone was waiting to hear my answer.

I put on my best high-class voice. "I want to visit the powder room."

That made everyone laugh, too, just like I'd hoped. Walking out into the bushes also gave me a little time to think.

I knew one thing: I wasn't having sex with Josh tonight. That was the path to nowhere, not to mention that the idea of it made me want to throw up. He was okay sober, not great, but okay. Drunk, he was definitely not my type.

A little privacy in his car might be the way to bargain toward an invitation to the dance. But it might also get me in trouble, because Josh was stronger than I was.

I tried to bring to mind the image of my mom

to give me courage. But all I could picture was her looking around for the photographer while her husband talked to her like she was a child. It didn't give me the courage I needed.

Still not sure what to do, I headed back toward the warmth of the bonfire, but before I reached the clearing, Tracey blocked my path. "Don't do it, girlfriend," she said.

"Do what?"

"Get in a car with Josh."

I didn't like being told what to do. "What's it to you?"

She shook her head. "It's nothing to me what that jerk does," she said. "Just a friendly warning."

Hmmm. That was the second friendly warning I'd had about Josh. "Thanks," I said.

"Hey, Sweet Piece," said one of Josh's friends, grabbing Tracey by the shoulder and spinning her around. "I thought we had a date."

"You call this a date?" she asked, but she went with him.

I shook my head. I could never understand girls who let guys dominate them.

Somehow, that decided me. Tracey might have had her problems in cars alone with boys, but she was obviously suffering from low self-esteem. And Kelly might have warned me about Josh, but she was way too nice to stand up for herself.

I wasn't like them. I was a strong woman, out to get what I wanted. I was a lot smarter than Josh, and I wasn't drunk. I could handle him. I knew I could.

When I walked out into the clearing, I saw that one of the girls who'd come with Tracey was leaning into Josh. He'd put his arm around her, but he was watching where I'd gone.

The moment he saw me, he spoke up. "Are we goin' or not?"

"Sure," I said.

He shoved the girl off him and headed toward his car, clicking his mouth like you'd call a dog. "This way."

I stood my ground. "Excuse me?"

"My car's this way." The word "this" came out "thish."

"I know where your car is," I said. "I'm just waiting to be invited with some respect."

"Gimme a break," he said.

I just stood there, one hand on my hip, watching him.

Someone threw another log on the fire and sparks flew up into the trees. Smoke blew into my eyes, making them water, but I didn't turn away.

"Suck it up, Josh," said one of his friends. "The lady has standards."

I let a tiny smile show.

Josh came over to me and held out his hand. "Will you come?"

Score one for me, I thought. And followed him to his car.

Chapter Twelve

Once we were alone in the backseat of the car, my heart started jumping, and not from lust. Josh had a self-satisfied look that said he'd got me just where he wanted me.

I tried to get my head in the game. It was the do-or-die moment in my campaign to get Josh. But part of me just wanted to get out, now.

"So," I said, to make conversation, "is this your car?"

"Yeah." He put his arm around me and pulled me close.

"Buy it yourself?" I asked, keeping my tone peppy and unromantic.

"No, my dad bought it for me when I got the tri-state football award." He started nuzzling my neck. "Baby, you're so sexy."

I tried to tame my sick-to-my-stomach feeling. Back where I'd lived before, Nate and I had spent plenty of time making out, and I loved it. We could hardly wait to be alone, and the feel of his big hands, the smell of his body, had made me hot.

With Josh, I felt cold as an ice sculpture.

Unfortunately, he was warming up. He kissed me, or at least tried to: He made his little wet tongue into a point and poked it between my lips.

Eeuw! I turned away before I could remind myself of all the reasons I ought to give Josh a little affection, at least.

My rejection of his kisses didn't seem to bother him. His real target was my chest. He grabbed the hem of my sweater and tugged at it.

"Hey!" I jerked away. "What do you think you're doing?"

"Getting you excited." He groped me with about as much finesse as a two-year-old grabbing toys off a shelf.

I almost laughed at his piss-poor technique. This was the stud of Linden High? I'd better hurry up and move toward my goal, or I was going to lose it, and lose everything I wanted, too.

I tried to think like Josh. He seemed like the kind of guy who'd expect some action when he took a girl somewhere nice. "Look," I said, shoving his hands away, "you haven't even taken me out. What gives you the right to feel me up?"

His hands came right back. "I'll take you out," he said, breathing hard.

"You'll take me out where?" I asked, grabbing him by his wrists.

"To a movie." He aimed a kiss my way again, and ended up slobbering down my cheek.

"I can take myself to a movie, Josh."

"Where you wanna go?" He was steaming up the windows with his hot, beer-scented breath.

I shifted away from him. Now or never. "I want you to take me to the Fall Dance."

"Aw, babe." His hands came toward me again.

"I'm serious."

"I don't know who I'm gonna—"

"Hands off, then. I'm getting out." I scooted over toward the car door.

"Okay," he said. "I'll take you." And he pulled me back toward him.

"You're not just saying that?"

"I said, I'll take you!" He sounded hot and bothered.

I leaned back against him, trying to ignore his awkward attempts to unhook my bra from outside my sweater. I wanted to relish my victory. I'd gotten an invite to the Fall Dance! From Josh Johnson! I'd be up there on the stage as Fall Queen, while my mother looked on and got impressed and decided she wanted to take me back!

Josh finally realized my bra didn't hook in the back and brought his hands around to try to find the front clasp. "Oh, babe, are you getting hot yet?" he panted somewhere near my neck.

"Not really." I tried to focus on the image of myself on the stage, to rise above the uncomfortable, invasive feel of his hands. It was hard to stay focused on anything good while he pawed at me.

I also felt small and dirty and fake. I didn't believe girls owed guys anything for a date. But here I was, trading a feel of my chest for an invitation to a dance. What did that make me?

When he finally pulled his hands off me and sat back, it was a huge relief.

Until I saw him go for the snap on his pants.

"What are you doing?" I heard the panicked squeal in my own voice, but I didn't care. I just wanted him to stay buttoned up.

"You know what I want you to do," he said, grabbing my hand and pulling it toward him.

Oh, please. I just about gagged. My hands pulled away from him before I could even think it through.

"C'mon, baby. I told you I'd take you to the dance. Now you have to give me something." He grabbed my hand again.

"No!" I pulled back and vaulted myself toward the door of the car.

I couldn't touch him. No way.

I fumbled for the door handle but couldn't find it. And then all of a sudden, Josh was pulling my legs so that I sprawled across the seat.

And then he was on top of me.

Fear flooded my body as his weight crushed me into the car seat. He fumbled with the opening of my jeans with one hand while his other arm held me down.

"Let me go!" I turned my face away from his beery kisses and got a whiff of his armpit that made me gag. Both of us were panting. I pushed at his chest, but it was like trying to move a stone wall.

"How d'ya get these open?" Josh was still pulling at the waist of my jeans. Thank heavens for tight ones. Thank heavens for Susan, who'd taken away all my short skirts.

I kept trying to push him and wiggle free, but he was strong. My heart raced double time. What had I gotten myself into? And could I get out?

Fear that I couldn't made me keep fighting, and thinking.

He had to let go of my arms to work on the snap, and I reached up and grabbed the door handle and shoved the car door open.

"Help! Help me, somebody!" I yelled as loudly as I could.

"Oh, you love this." Josh seemed totally unworried, which scared me. Didn't he care what his friends thought? Weren't his friends the kind of people who'd help a girl under attack?

"Hey, help me out here!" I yelled even louder than before. "He's trying to rape me! Somebody call the cops!"

And then I started clawing and shoving and using my knees to try to get him off me.

Josh snarled and tugged at my jeans, sliding his fingers under the waistband.

I held my breath, took aim, and gave him a knee-bang right where it counted.

"Ow!" He arched away and I scooted out from underneath him. I slid partway out of the car, my hands trying to find purchase on the wet, sharp gravel.

He dove toward me and I kicked my legs wildly, like I was swimming, and landed hard on the ground. It hurt, but the cold damp air felt like freedom.

"So you like to fight, do you?" Josh's voice came from the car door above me, and then he threw his body over mine.

Gravel dug into my head and my back where my top didn't meet my jeans. Josh was heavy on me, like a giant stone.

A stone with strong, groping arms.

"Hey," I yelled, but now my voice was hoarse, pathetic with tears.

Josh rolled to the side and went for his own buttons again, still holding me down with one leg and one arm.

All of a sudden, I saw something dark over us, and then Josh doubled over and gave a yelp of pain.

"C'mon!" said a girl's voice, and I felt a tug at my arm. "Let's get outta here!"

Chapter Thirteen

It was Tracey, helping me up and half-pushing, half-carrying me to her car. She shoved me in the front seat and I collapsed, too weak even to fix my clothes. Somewhere I heard yelling, but I was too limp to care.

I'd never felt so low. Here I was in this hick town, trying to get along, trying to get into the social scene, and look what happened. I about got raped, something worse than had ever happened to me in my foster homes in the city.

I had no one to care about me, no one to really help me. So I'd tried to help myself, with my big, stupid plan about Josh Johnson.

Now I had nothing.

Outside the car I heard Tracey yelling, and then she got in and started it up. We roared out of there.

"You wanna go to the cops?" she asked.

I shook my head. No local cop was going to take my side against the football hero, and all Josh's friends would say I'd gotten into the car willingly. I knew I didn't have a case.

"Home?"

I shook my head. "I gotta clean up first." I looked down at my dirty clothes and saw that Josh had ripped a hole in the front of my sweater.

Tracey glanced over and shook her head. "He's some romantic lover," she said as she pulled the car into a driveway. "Come on. You can clean up at my house."

Later, after I'd slipped past Susan and Kelly and taken a long hot shower, I lay in bed and hugged my teddy bear and thought about my options.

Not only had I won and lost the chance to go with Josh to the Fall Dance, but I'd also killed my reputation at Linden High. Not that it was so great to begin with, but with as many people as had been at that party, I knew word of what happened would spread. I also knew the story would have Josh's spin on it.

That meant I would never get invited to the Fall Dance.

Ticket sales ended the next day. And when I remembered I was scheduled to sell tickets with Kelly, I curled my legs up into a fetal position and moaned.

How had things gone so bad so fast? Why had

I even let myself care about this stupid school and the things that went on there? Why hadn't I just run back to Nate and the city instead of trying to fit into Green Acres?

And why, oh why, had I so brilliantly invited my mother to the Fall Dance?

I was so cold. I couldn't stop shivering. My back ached, and my elbows stung where gravel had dug into them.

Even worse was how dirty I felt inside. I had to admit to myself that I'd gotten into the car, that I'd let Josh feel me up, that I'd bargained some of myself for an invitation to the dance. So even though I was furious at Josh, I was just as mad at myself.

When I walked into the cafeteria the next day, there was that funny little hush. Not like everyone in the room stopped talking and eating, but there were certain pockets of silence. I even thought I heard someone say, "Sssh, there she is!"

But I might have been imagining it. Especially after hearing whispers and giggles in my classes all morning.

I went toward the food area and scanned the deli section just to have something to do. Behind me, the noise level rose again: silverware against dishes, the dull roar of hundreds of talking, laughing, and yelling kids.

The smell of fried food and the steam from giant pans of macaroni and cheese made me feel sick. I turned away.

"Trinity! Over here!" Kelly beckoned from the table set up by the windows.

Just what I wanted, more attention called to me.

Out of habit, I put on my cockiest walk and headed over. "Nice display," I said to Kelly, nodding at the hand-lettered signs. "Dance Benefits Saint Helen's Home," said one. Another, with cute pictures of girls from the Saint Helen's brochures, read, "Have Fun While You Help Girls Like Us."

"How about this one?" she said, pointing to the larger-than-life cutout of a guy's fist, with "I didn't mean to hit her" in a thought-bubble above. The heading was *Esteem Is Essential*. "I figured you'd like it."

I didn't meet her eyes. "Cool."

She grabbed my arm, pulled me behind the table, and hissed, "Why didn't you tell me what happened?"

"What?" I shook her hand off my arm.

"Josh."

It figured that she'd heard. She and everyone else in the school. "Maybe I didn't feel like talking about it," I said. "Just like maybe I don't feel like sitting here in front of everybody selling tickets."

"What else are you gonna do, sit by yourself?" she asked. "Or sit with Josh and his friends while they talk about you?"

I took a quick scan of the cafeteria. Sure

enough, there was Josh at the so-called head table, not twenty feet away, surrounded by his fellow football players and a bunch of cheerleader-type girls.

The sight of him made me want to hide. How come he could look all happy and carefree while every step I took felt like a chore? How come nobody was pointing and whispering about him?

"Did you really have sex with him and then cry rape?" Kelly asked.

My head jerked around toward her. "Is that what he's saying?"

She nodded.

A surge of heat rose from my heart to the top of my head. "I could kill him. Right now. I'm gonna go over there and curse him out."

Kelly put a hand on my arm. "Don't. He's got a lot more friends than you do." And then, to my complete surprise, she put her arm around me. "Oh, Trinity, did he really rape you?" Her voice was all quivery, and when I looked at her, I saw tears in her eyes.

Good God, the girl was acting like she actually cared about me. "No, I'm okay," I said.

"Are you sure?" An angry flush spread across her cheekbones. "I know how he can put the pressure on."

"Yeah, well, he put the pressure on me pretty bad at that party. But I got out, thanks to Tracey."

"Tracey the slut?"

"Hey, that's my girl you're talking about. She saved my butt and she's cool."

Kelly raised her eyebrows, but some kids came up then to buy tickets. I got busy and tried to ignore the whispers and glances my way. I took deep breaths to keep from strangling Josh. I also tried not to think about the dance and how I wouldn't be going.

A fairly popular senior guy bought tickets while his new sophomore girlfriend stood behind him. A couple minutes later she came back. "What are the rules for the Fall King and Queen?" she asked.

Kelly gave her a pitying look. "Everyone votes when they come in," she explained.

"It's by the couple?"

"That's right."

"Ooh, I have a chance!" The girl looked thrilled as she scurried back to her friends to spread the news.

"You wish," Kelly said under her breath.

"Who d'ya think it's going to be?" Kelly's friend Joan asked. She was hanging around by the table as if she might get a date that way. "Do you still think it'll be Josh, even after . . ." She shot a glance at me and blushed.

"Sure," Kelly said. "Look at him. His reputation is better than ever."

Sure enough, even more girls were draped on the guys around Josh's table. He appeared to be holding court.

Some of them noticed we were looking their way and started nudging each other. "Hey, Trinity," called a guy, not a football jock, but a wannabe. "How come you're working for a feminazi cause? Rough night last night?"

"She's working for Saint Helen's because she's got a kind heart and wants to help other people, unlike you," Kelly snapped before I could begin to wrap my tongue around a reply.

Once again, I was surprised. The girl had my back.

Lonnie strolled up and I was glad. A guy who respected girls. A guy who cared about me.

"This, mates, is temptation," he said to no one in particular. "The two most gorgeous women in the school selling tickets to the dance."

"Aw, you're just talking," Kelly said, her cheeks pink.

"Lonnie's a big talker," I told her.

"I wonder if he's all talk, no action?" she said, looking at him.

"That, my dear, sounds like a challenge," he said. "Two tickets, please."

My heart did a little jump in my chest. Who was Lonnie taking to the dance?

And wouldn't it be fun to go with him?

Of course, going to the dance with Lonnie, I wouldn't impress my mom. But on a day like this, it would feel so good to be asked. To be wanted. To be liked for who I really was.

Kelly had handed him the tickets and had her silly pink-feather pen poised over our list. "Who are you taking?"

"Well, I assume the two of you are spoken for—"

"No," I said.

"I thought I was," said Kelly.

He'd opened his mouth to say something, but now he glanced at me. "Did you say no?"

I nodded.

He turned back toward Kelly, so I did too. She was looking at him, a little smile on her face, one eyebrow cocked.

He took a deep breath in and let it out. Then he smiled at Kelly. "You know who I'm taking."

I frowned. Had he assumed I'd say yes?

"Yeah, I know, unless you were jaggin' me yesterday." She started writing.

I watched that pink feather bob. And then I leaned over to read what she'd written.

She wrote, *Lonnie Mason / Kelly Turner.*

Bam! I felt like I'd been socked in the gut. So much so that I actually crossed my arms over my stomach and leaned forward.

Lonnie . . . and Kelly?

Why hadn't I known?

And why did it hurt so much?

Kelly gave him an adorable little smile and said, "Remember, no corsages. You donate the money you would've spent on flowers to the shelter.

We'll have an anti-flower collection bin right inside the door."

"What if I find a way to bring you flowers *and* support the cause?"

"No way," Kelly said. "We're turning away anyone at the door who's wearing a corsage."

"But if you're the one who makes the rules, can't you bend them?" He was leaning over the table between us.

"I have to set an example," she said with a stern little shake of her finger.

"Oh, no, a high-minded date. What was I thinking?" He slid into a chair on the other side of Kelly and started talking to her in a low voice, saying things that made her giggle and turn red.

I squeezed the fold between my thumb and forefinger as hard as I could in the hopes that the pain would distract me.

I desperately wanted to leave. I didn't want to watch them flirt anymore.

I'd thought Lonnie only talked with me like that. Had it all been a silly game, one he played with any girl who'd listen to him?

The lunch hour was nearing an end, at least. I'd be able to get out of here and cry.

Ticket sales would be over.

And, clearly, I wasn't going to get a last-minute invite.

Just when I thought things couldn't get any worse, Josh swaggered over. He was alone, but all his friends were watching from their nearby table.

So were at least half of the rest of the kids in the cafeteria. Obviously, the story about Josh and me had spread all over school, and people were watching to see how we'd interact.

My heart pounded with a mix of rage and fear. I couldn't forget the feeling of him on top of me, his strong arms pushing me down, his hands groping everywhere. Even though we were surrounded by people, I felt like it could happen again. My body jazzed up with adrenaline, telling me to run away.

But my brain refused to even look away from Josh, let alone run away. He was the one who did something wrong, not me. He was the criminal, and we both knew it, even if we both also knew the case wouldn't stand up in court.

His swagger got more pronounced as he approached. "He-e-ey, Trinity," he said in a voice that suggested we shared a secret.

I gave him my best sneer. "What?"

"I need a couple of tickets," he said.

Well, of course. And I didn't have any choice but to sell them to him, even if it made me sick. I looked over to Kelly, hoping for an assist, but she was leaning over a book with Lonnie and didn't seem to have noticed Josh's presence.

Growling to myself, I got him the tickets and pulled out the list. "Who are you going with?" I asked.

He didn't answer, and when I looked up, he was looking back at his buddies with a big grin on his face.

Then he looked at me and said, "Don't you know, Trinity?"

"I don't know, and I don't care," I said. My jaw was so tight the words came out like the voice of a robot. And that was how I felt, too: like I was on automatic, functioning even though my heart and soul were crying inside.

"You cared last night," he said in a stage whisper.

The guys at his table broke up laughing.

I stood up, put my hands on my hips, and gave the table a glare that said they were nothing but maggots, maggots feeding off the deathly Josh Johnson.

Most of them stopped laughing.

Josh wasn't intimidated. I guess the fact that he'd had his hands all over me made him bold. "You mentioned you were looking for a date for the dance," he said loudly. "Are you still waiting?"

I looked him in the eyes. "I'm not waiting for you, if that's what you're asking," I said.

He faked a shoulder-slump. "Aw, you're killing me, Trinity. Don't tell me that once was enough?"

I kept my eyes trained on his, but I could feel my legs starting to shake. I wanted to slap the leer off his handsome face. I wanted to crawl under the table and cry. Most of all, I wanted a friend.

But I'd never felt so alone.

Some of the guys were laughing loudly as they looked my way. Obviously they were making jokes at my expense. Other kids were watching. It felt like everyone was watching.

And for once, I was at a loss for words.

"Hey!" said a girl's voice, even louder than Josh. "Trinity, what gives? Are you still talking to Josh after the crap he pulled on you last night?"

It was Tracey, and her comment—plus her trademark cheap polyester miniskirt, black fishnet stockings, and four-inch heels—took the spotlight off me for the minute I needed.

I found my smile and my strength looking into her sympathetic eyes. Here was a girl who'd been called "slut" forever, according to Kelly, and still kept her head up high.

"No kidding," I said in an equally loud voice. "From kissing to groping, he's clueless. He couldn't even find the hook on my bra, not that his style of loving made me want to take it off."

Tracey nodded thoughtfully. "Wonder how come he can still get dates?" she said into the silence. "Or maybe that's why he dates so many girls. In his case, once *is* enough."

"Once is too much. Look at this." I shoved up the sleeve of my sweater to show my scraped-up arm.

Beside me, I heard Kelly gasp.

"I'm just glad I kept my clothes on," I added. "I needed the padding when he shoved me down and jumped me."

"Maybe the poor guy doesn't realize the cave man approach is out of style," Tracey said.

"Didn't do much for me," I agreed.

Neither of us had cracked a smile this whole time. Instinctively, we'd kept talking like we didn't realize people were listening, but twice as loud as normal.

Aside from our voices, the cafeteria was utterly silent.

Kelly cleared her throat and pulled out her pink-feathered pen. "Who's the, um, lucky girl you're taking to the dance, Josh?"

The whole room broke up laughing and jeering, his jock friends the loudest of all. Josh was red-faced and speechless. And one of the cheerleaders who'd been perched on his table now looked distinctly unhappy.

He mumbled a name to Kelly and slunk away as the bell rang.

Lonnie whistled. "Remind me not to get on the bad side of you three," he said.

Kelly started gathering up the ticket materials. "All right, that's it. Sales are over," she said.

"You going?" Tracey asked me.

"Nah. No date."

"You don't have to have a date to go," Tracey said. "A lot of people go stag."

I looked over at Kelly. She was shaking her head. "The only people who go stag are . . ."

"What?" Tracey asked with a dangerous smile.

Kelly blushed.

Tracey glared at her.

"What?" I asked. "Geeks from the honors program? Girls everyone calls 'slut'? Unpopular kids who can't get a date?"

"Well," Kelly said. "Yeah."

I shrugged. "I qualify, then. Give me a ticket."

Chapter Fourteen

After buying my solo ticket to the Fall Dance, I felt a compelling urge to crawl into a hole and stay there. What had I been thinking?

Kelly wouldn't let me alone, though. "Would you get off that computer and talk to me?" she asked that night, coming out of her bedroom into our study for the third time.

I'd just noticed something different about the ALTLIVES screen and I wanted to check it out. But Kelly was looming over me and I didn't want her to see what I was doing.

ALTLIVES was my only private thing, and I wanted to keep it that way.

"What d'you want?" I asked as I shrunk the window. "I'm busy. I have homework."

"First, I want to know if you're okay about whatever it was that happened with Josh."

Lee McClain

"I'm okay," I said. "And it's over, and I don't want to talk about it."

She leaned against the wall, arms crossed, studying me. "If he did anything to you, Mom will press charges," she said.

"He scared me and embarrassed me, but that's not illegal," I said. "I got away. And anyway, I embarrassed him right back today."

"Yeah, that was great," she said. She picked up a book and put it back on the shelf. "Hey, Trin. What's Lonnie really like?"

My feeling of being close to Kelly evaporated. The thought of her and Lonnie together made a bad taste rise in my mouth. "You should know," I said. "You're dating him, right?"

"Not really. He just asked me to the dance."

"When did he first talk to you about it?" I didn't want to seem overly interested, but I felt like I had to know.

"Yesterday," she said. "It's pretty last-minute. I wonder how many girls turned him down first. He didn't ask you, did he?"

I thought about our hot conversation in the alcove. "No," I said. "He didn't ask me."

"So what's he like? You're in class with him. Spill it, Trinity. Please!"

I did a heavy sigh. "Okay. He's smart. Funny. Kinda sexy, I think."

"Me too," she said.

"He's in some international soccer club in the

city. So he knows all these people from all over the place. Plus, he's actually got good muscles even though he's so skinny."

"Yeah, I saw," Kelly said.

"And he doesn't care what people think of him, so he's a bit of an outcast." I tipped back the desk chair so I could see her better. "In fact, I'm surprised you're going with him. He's not exactly in your crowd."

"Yeah, but nobody else asked me," she said. "And he was so funny about it, so outrageous. Telling me how beautiful I am and all. He's like a guy on TV."

I'd heard enough. "I really need to get some stuff done," I said, turning back to the computer screen, hoping she'd take a hint.

She didn't. "It'll be hard on you going to the dance alone," she said. "I know some kids do it, but . . ."

"But not your friends. I know."

"Who'll you sit with? Who'll you talk to? I mean, you can hang out with me and Lonnie, but . . ."

"Don't worry about it," I said. "I'm a big girl, and I've been on my own a long time. I can handle a dance at Podunk High."

"I hate it when you call us that."

I shrugged. "The truth can hurt."

"Okay, fine," she said, and went downstairs.

I felt worse, not better. Kelly was right; the dance would be a drag. And watching Kelly dance with Lonnie wasn't going to bring me a lot of joy.

I escaped into ALTLIVES. As soon as I popped up the window, I saw what was different about the screen: there was a new icon on it.

Of course, I clicked right away.

Congratulations! the screen proclaimed. *You have logged enough hours for the ALTLIVES Switch.* Then the words faded away and a scene came on.

It opened on video with no sound, but it wasn't Mom's luxury digs. Instead, I focused in on a familiar-looking counter covered in black Formica, blue vinyl stools lined up along it, and a couple of biker-type guys smoking cigarettes.

And there was Mom in the same waitress uniform she'd worn right before giving me away.

Was the game taking me into the way-back machine?

But as I studied Mom, I saw that she was older than I remembered her. Her uniform was tighter, and not in a good way. She looked a little bit fat. There were lines on her face, and gray roots showed through a bad dye job.

Was it the future? Had Mom lost everything?

I watched as she did the same things I'd grown up seeing her do. Only now I understood them better. When she leaned close to the men at the counter, I saw that she was showing them some skin. I wanted to yell, "But they're losers! Don't give it up for them!"

Of course, I didn't. I knew she couldn't hear me.

When the two guys left—throwing down only a dollar tip between them, the cheapskates—Mom wandered back to the break room and picked up a magazine. It was some star rag with a picture of Gennifer Joline in her latest movie. I'd seen it last week.

That shook me up because I realized: this scene was present-day.

What was Mom doing back in the crappy bar and grill she'd worked at years ago? Was she sneaking out to get to her old life? And why did she look so much uglier now than she had the last time I'd seen her?

Another waitress came into the room, and I switched to the transcript so I could hear what they were saying.

"Hey," says the seated waitress.

"You got a phone call from the school again," says the other waitress.

"Oh, cripes," says the seated waitress. "They still on the line?"

The other woman shakes her head. "They want you to come pick up your kid. I told 'em you'd be there."

Lee McClain

The first waitress drops her head into her hand. "Man, I'm tired."

"That Trinity's a handful, ain't she?"

I froze. Trinity? The bad kid at the school was me?

"Yeah, she's a piece of work. Just like I was." The seated waitress shakes her head. "She gets more like me every day." She stands up. "Better move before Walt gets back. He's been on my case about my hours."

I stared at the transcript as the meaning of the game dawned on me.

This was what our lives would've been like if she hadn't given me up. This was the alternate life.

She wouldn't have married the rich guy. We'd still live in that same one-bedroom apartment, most likely, and she'd still work at Walt's Bar.

And I'd be a kid in trouble.

But I'd be with my mom. And getting more like her every day, according to her.

All of a sudden an instant message box came up on the screen.

ALTLIFE! Do you choose to switch over?

There was a place to check "no" or "yes."

Behind the box, the transcript was gone. Instead, I was watching my mom get into an old beater of a car and drive a few blocks to a school, one I vaguely remembered from our old neighborhood.

Another line flashed in the box: *Your choice option will time out in five minutes.*

My head was spinning. Was this what I thought it was? Was it a chance to switch over into a different life, my old life, as if nothing had ever happened? As if Mom had never given me up?

My heart pounded and my palms sweated as I checked the clock in the corner of the computer screen. 8:56 P.M.

I watched as Mom walked into the building, through security, and into the office. She seemed familiar with the routine; she went up and signed something before even turning to look at the row of seats for students in trouble.

And there I was.

My hair was frizzy-wild and I was wearing such a short skirt that I almost blushed. Susan would never have let me get away with it, and I wondered if I'd snuck out of the house, if Mom would say anything. But she just beckoned to me and turned to leave the office.

I got up and walked out of there with a strut and an attitude that should have gotten me expelled.

Once outside the building, she lit into me. I couldn't hear any of the words, but I could see the anger on her face and the sassy look on mine. She was pointing at her watch and gesturing toward the car.

I took my good old time walking to it, but when I got there, she shoved me in hard. We continued to yell at one another all the way back to the bar and as we made our way inside, too.

All of a sudden I remembered the time and checked. Nine o'clock. I had to decide right now. Did I want to switch back to my life with Mom? Did I want to be the poor-trash child of a miserable waitress . . . but a regular, normal biological child living with my mom? Or did I want the nice bedroom, the computer, Kelly, Susan?

"Hey Trin." Kelly flounced by. "Mom wants to see you downstairs."

"I'm busy."

"She said *now.* She's, quote, *concerned* about your going to the dance alone."

On the screen, Walt-the-manager had come out and was yelling at Mom. Again, I couldn't hear the words, but I saw the attitude pasted on her face and how it was the mirror image of my own. I saw my alter ego step in front of Mom and say something to the manager.

I saw Mom hide a grin—and then slap my face.

Wow! As I watched my on-screen self turn away, crying, my heart was pounding. Did I want to stay in this life, or to switch over? I couldn't decide. But I had to.

A burly customer came by. On his way to a booth, he put a casual hand on Mom's butt.

I expected her to slap him. Instead, she gave him a big smile.

I watched her shoulders slump as the guy continued to his booth without talking to her. Walt kept on yelling.

I moved the cursor to the choice box on the screen and clicked "no."

Immediately the screen went black.

And I was left with a cruel, bitter ache in my heart. I'd had a chance to be with my mom. To never have been a foster kid. To wipe out all the hurt of the past eight years.

And I'd turned it down.

I put my head down on the keyboard and my mind went as black as the screen.

After I'd maxed out on self-pity, I sat up, grabbed some tissue, and cleaned myself up. I tried to give myself a pep talk. *This just means that I really, really have to make the dance an occasion to impress her and convince her to take me back, now that her life is better.*

But without a date, let alone a chance at Fall Queen, how was I going to do it?

Chapter Fifteen

Driving toward Saint Helen's was like taking a trip down memory lane.

There was the corner store where I'd shop-lifted a pack of cigarettes for my mom and gotten caught. There was the bench where Nate and I had shared our first kiss.

There was the front porch of Saint Helen's, where Mom had brought me almost eight years before.

I scanned the neighborhood as Susan parked the car. We were surrounded by row houses with boarded-up windows and apartment buildings with gazillions of little kids playing in front. Guys hung out in front of a car wash across the street. Music thumped from boom boxes and car stereos.

"Is this, like, the ghetto?" Kelly asked

"This is, like, my old stomping grounds," I said.

We were here to meet the girls from Saint

Helen's and figure out an appropriate use for the two thousand dollars we intended to donate. At least, that was the official purpose.

For me, it was a test. Saint Helen's was the place where I'd spent my first few months after Mom left, and where I'd come every time one of my foster placements had ended during those first two years before I ended up at the Holmsteads.

It was rank and old and the food was nasty, but in an odd way, it was home.

And on the plus side, it was in my old neighborhood. Ever since I'd turned down the ALTLIVES switch, I'd been thinking about coming back.

I knew I could find a way to wreck the placement with Susan and get sent back here. Was that what I wanted to do?

Kelly half-tripped on the cracked concrete steps that led up to the porch. "This place is ratty," she complained.

Susan pushed at the doorbell.

"It's broken," I said, guessing that in eight years they'd never gotten it fixed.

"Seems to be," agreed Susan, and started knocking.

Memories flooded over me. Mom and I had stood forever on this porch, on a cold rainy day exactly like this, waiting for someone to come. I'd been just big enough to see through the windows to the other girls staring out at me.

I hadn't been big enough to keep from crying,

though. Mom didn't yell at me like she usually did, but after a while she put her gloved hands up over her ears to shut out the sound. Neither one of us had a tissue, so when someone finally answered her pounding, my face was a mess of tears and snot.

"Take her," Mom had said, and tried to turn around and leave before anyone could see that she was crying too. But the old nun who ran the place at that time had made her come in and sign papers and talk for a long time.

The way I'd felt those first hours and days still hollowed out my insides some nights. It made me wrap my arms around myself even today, here, in this awful spot.

Susan kept knocking on the door, and finally a dark black woman answered and ushered us inside. She was tall and thin, with cheekbones to die for and close-cropped hair. "So you're the ones who organized this help for us," she said, her clipped accent betraying an island origin. "We are most thankful. Why don't you come meet our girls?"

It wasn't an offer, but an order, and we all fell into line behind her. When we got to the recreation room, the place was noisy with teenage girls: some sitting at a table studying, some learning a dance routine, and some playing pool. A doorway across the room led toward a hall of offices.

The tall woman clapped her hands, and the noise in the recreation room died down.

"Ladies," she said, "here are two girls from Linden High School, the ones who are making a major donation for us. I want you to make them welcome. Maybe together, you teenagers can come up with the right use for the money."

"Party!" called one of the girls.

"I expect some serious thinking and a useful collaboration."

"Yo, Miss Nadine," one of the girls called. "What's collaboration?"

"Working together, stupid," said a small, intense-looking Hispanic girl I thought I recognized from somewhere.

"Working together with respect, Esperanza." Miss Nadine cocked her head to one side. "Understand?"

Esperanza nodded with just a touch of insolence in her stare.

Susan and Miss Nadine walked toward the hallway of offices. Kelly and I stood together, looking at the Saint Helen's girls.

Most of them had gone back to whatever they had been doing. The game of pool continued. In a corner I hadn't noticed before, a girl sat staring into nowhere, tears running down her face. She was pretty as an angel, blond and pink. And she was so pregnant she looked about to pop.

I shook my head. Without even asking, I felt like I knew her story.

Three younger girls were there, playing hairdo with a couple of the teenagers. I remembered that from when I'd stayed here the first time. The big girls would often invite some of the little ones in to play.

One of the little girls looked sad. She also looked about eight, the age I'd been when I first came. I went over to her.

"Hi," I said. "What's your name?"

"She don't talk," said one of the teenagers.

"Can't or won't?" I asked, smiling at her.

"We don't know," the same girl answered. "She just came a couple of weeks ago. Ain't said a word so far."

The girl looked at me with searching, soulful eyes. I knew what she was searching for, and I knew I didn't have it to give. I wasn't her mother.

And what kind of mother would leave a sweet, sad child like that?

Behind me, I heard Kelly clear her throat in a weird way. I'd forgotten her for a moment, but she had to be flipping out. There were only a few other white girls here, and none who looked prissy and suburban like her.

I touched the little girl's hair and then turned toward Kelly. She was talking to a small group of girls. It didn't look friendly.

"Why do you want to raise money for us?" Esperanza was asking her.

Kelly shrugged. "Mom made us do a service project."

Esperanza laughed. "Just what I always wanted to be, a service project."

Kelly blushed and looked at me.

"Come on," I said to the room rather than to anyone in particular. "We have about ten minutes to figure out what to do with two thousand dollars."

"I can think of things," Esperanza said.

"Yeah, but you heard Miss Nadine," said another girl. "It's got to be worthwhile."

A heavyset girl with freckles groaned. "Another service project? I thought *we* were the ones who needed help, not the ones who had to do for others all the time!"

Some girls who'd been playing pool and talking low broke in. "How about a party?" a petite one said. "We could throw a real nice party for that kind of money. A dance, even."

"Mom says it has to relate to self-esteem." Kelly said.

"Yeah, God forbid the poor foster girls should have fun," Esperanza grumbled.

"We could make it fun," I started to say.

"What do you mean, *we?*" sneered Esperanza. "You two won't be involved. You just come in here to show off. Then you'll go back to your fancy high school."

I gave her a look. "Don't take your mad out on us, girlfriend. I've done my time here."

"You what?" She stared at me, and then recognition dawned. "Hey, I think I know you."

"Trinity B. Jones," I said. "Lived here a couple of years ago."

"We crossed paths, I think," she said.

"You between placements?"

She rolled her eyes. "Yeah, but I hope never to go back to a foster home. I'm so sick of fighting off my so-called brothers in those places. I'd rather be here just with girls."

"I hear you."

Kelly was staring at us. "That's really awful," she said. "Maybe we should use the money for, like, counseling for you guys."

"Yeah, well, I'd rather have a good course in karate." Esperanza got a dangerous grin on her face.

"Hey," I said, "that's not a bad idea."

"It's a great idea," Kelly said, to my surprise. "I know, when Josh was trying to, you know . . ." She trailed off. "I could've used some better moves."

I stared at her. "It got that bad?"

She shrugged. "He was holding me down and ripping at my clothes," she said.

I blew out a sigh and shook my head. "Sounds way too familiar."

Esperanza cocked her head to one side. "Let me get this straight," she said to me. "You got out of this dump and went to live someplace great, with rich people. And you still got the same problems?" She frowned. "You coming back here?"

I looked around the roomful of girls. I did like the life and color here. I liked it that these girls were survivors like me. I liked that they had compassion for the little ones who came in. I liked them better than a lot of the girls in Linden Falls.

Kelly spoke up. "No, Trinity's not coming back here! We're adopting her." And then she clapped her hand over her mouth.

I looked at her with my eyebrows raised high. "You want to explain?"

"I'm not supposed to tell you until Mom talks to you," she said.

"Oh, come on," said Esperanza. "Tell us about it." She had the look of a little girl begging for a fairy tale.

That brought to mind something I hadn't thought of in years. Back when I lived here, we all loved stories about kids getting adopted by some rich person. We all clustered around the rare older kid who'd found a permanent family, begging for details, imagining ourselves in the starring role.

I'd stopped doing it when I realized no one wanted to adopt teenagers. At that point, the only dream left was my mom.

Kelly shrugged. "There's not much to tell," she said. "Mom and I have been talking, that's all. It's not like Trinity is perfect or anything, but we've kind of gotten used to having her around."

Her words made something swirl in my chest. I'd been working so hard to try to impress my real mom that I hadn't even thought of trying to impress Kelly and Susan. And yet they wanted me.

Esperanza gave me a funny look and then scanned the room. "Yo, ladies," she said. "We gonna spend the money on self-defense classes."

"That's no fun," said another girl.

"Yeah, and it ain't cooperative."

"Collaborative," said Esperanza. "Well, we could invite the rich white girls to come. It sounds like they need it."

"And you guys could come to our Fall Dance," I said, surprising myself. But I meant it. I wanted some of this life and color out there.

One of the girls started dancing around. "Like I said before, par-tee," she chanted.

"Any cute guys out your way?" the heavyset, freckled girl asked.

I sucked my lips. City girls were used to going to dances stag and hooking up there. At Linden High, couples were the thing.

"Lonnie's cute," Kelly said brightly.

"Yeah, easy for you to say. He's your date."

"He got any friends?" Esperanza asked.

"You know . . ." Kelly began.

"His soccer club!" I said, and we slapped hands. "We can invite them!"

Another girl who'd been listening came over. "There any black guys there?"

Kelly and I looked at each other. "There are guys from all over in this soccer club," Kelly said. "It's for international students. If we invite them, there'll be plenty of guys to go around."

"Of every color," I added.

It took about ten minutes and all of our efforts to talk Susan and Miss Nadine into it. But the Saint Helen's girls knew how to talk Miss Nadine's language, and there was a lot about collaboration and cooperation and community service. Meanwhile, Kelly and I worked on Susan by harping on education and cultural exchange.

In the end, we got what we wanted. All the way home, I felt exhilarated by what we'd accomplished.

It was later that the doubts crept in. I just wasn't sure how a whole gang of street-smart girls and international boys would work out at Linden High.

And I wasn't sure how they'd play in front of my mom.

Chapter Sixteen

There were lights. There were cameras.

And in just a few minutes, it looked like there'd be some action.

This had to be the first time so many brown-skinned girls had entered the hallowed halls of Linden High.

Add to that the fact that their dresses were a little more, well, spectacular than those of the small-town girls, and there was no way anyone would miss our entrance.

I say "our" because I was in among them, welcoming them and talking to them while the white kids stared. I'd borrowed a dress that was more along their lines than Kelly's, and I must admit, the red sequins and low-cut bodice showed me off.

I was sweating and half-sick. At the last minute, I'd come very close to bagging the whole thing. It wasn't going to be any fun at all to watch Lonnie and Kelly snuggle, to try to integrate the shelter girls into Linden High, or to watch Josh Johnson hold court.

One terrifying hope had made me come: I was about to see my mother. In person.

"Kelly, where have you been?" I recognized Trish's voice and spun to see that Lonnie and Kelly had just walked in the door.

Lonnie looked awesome in his suit, and Kelly was beautiful and wholesome-looking, too. Seeing the two of them smile together for the photographer snapping candids made me ache a little more inside.

When was it going to be my turn to have a nice, simple date with someone who respected me and was also cute and fun? Why was everything I did so complicated?

Kelly and Lonnie were over on one side of the reception area, which was decorated with pumpkins and cornstalks.

The girls and I were on the other side, talking and looking and being looked at.

I craned around to see if any of Lonnie's friends from the international club had shown up.

Instead, I saw my mother.

She swept in the door on the arm of her husband, smashing in a bright red dress. When the photographer automatically snapped her picture, she stopped and gave a gracious smile.

The greeters fussed with her little sable wrap and she spoke to them.

"Sure, Kelly Turner is here," the greeter said. "Kelly! This lady says she's a special guest."

Kelly, who'd been warned before that I had used her name to get the donor, but who didn't know why, went up and greeted Mom graciously. They talked for a minute while Mom's eyes skimmed the crowd in a way I recognized. She was looking for anyone important, and for anyone with a camera.

Her gaze skimmed right over me and my crowd of girls.

I quickly pointed the girls to where they could hang up their coats and freshen up. I should have taken them there myself, but I felt drawn to my mom like a hungry kid to a bakery window. Part of my hunger was withdrawal. After I'd checked the "no" box on the ALTLIVES screen, I hadn't even tried to spy on her. Virtual Mom just didn't do it for me anymore. I felt like I had to take my chances on the real thing.

I pushed through the crowd to hear what she was saying, making sure I stayed behind a couple of tall teachers. I wasn't ready for her to see me just yet. So I hovered toward the back of the small crowd that surrounded her and Kelly, listening.

"Some dress, Trinity," came a sarcastic voice behind me. It was Kelly's friend Stephanie. "You know, they do make clothes in your size."

I glanced at the innocuous peach-toned sheath that skimmed her size-four figure. "It must be rough having to shop in the little girls' department," I said with fake sympathy. "But don't worry. I'm sure you'll get a figure someday."

"My date is plenty happy with my figure," she said. "Where's yours?"

I just ignored her and took a step closer to Mom and Kelly. I didn't want to miss what they were saying.

"Here's the ballot box for the Fall King and Queen," Kelly was saying. "Each person who comes in gets to cast a ballot for one couple."

I'd already cast mine—for Kelly and Lonnie. I knew there wouldn't be many votes for them—they were such an odd couple from two different worlds—but if I looked around, they were the two people I liked best here. And family had to stick with family. Kelly was really starting to feel like a sister.

My jealousy felt like a sister's jealousy, too. I hated seeing her and Lonnie together.

Mom looked very animated as she studied the Fall King and Queen display. "So who are the leading contenders?" she asked. "How is it judged?"

Her obvious interest made me hurt inside. I'd read her exactly right. She loved the idea of an elected Fall King and Queen. That *would* have been the way to impress her.

I'd had my chance, and I'd blown it.

But would impressing my mom have made up for dating a lech?

All of a sudden the crowd noise took on a deeper tone, and when I turned to see why, I saw boys. Lots of boys. All ages from ours up to college, from the looks of things, and all the colors of the rainbow too.

That made me sigh with relief. At least the Saint Helen's girls would have some unattached boys to dance with. And so would I, if I even felt like dancing.

There was a clanking and bustle behind me, and I turned to see a local reporter and her camera guy. All right! Susan had helped us figure out ways to bring our event to the media's attention, but I hadn't really expected it to work.

Mom was going to love this.

"Where are the girls who put together the charity aspect of the dance?" the reporter was asking.

I glanced at Mom. She hadn't heard the question, but was angling herself for the most flattering photo.

"You might want to get a shot of that woman," I said to the reporter. "She's the major donor for the dance. We're having a ceremony in half an hour."

"Oh, sure," she said. "But I'm more interested in the teenagers."

Fortunately, when she met Mom a minute later,

she was all smiles and interested questions. She gave Mom a two-minute interview on camera.

Pretty soon it was time to get started. The first thing was to present a certificate to Mom. I was supposed to help with it, but at the last minute I got too shy and begged my way out of it. I didn't want Mom to realize who I was on a stage in front of a gym full of people, just in case there was some kind of teary reconciliation.

Besides, it was her chance to shine. She'd want the moment all to herself.

So I watched from the sidelines as Susan and Kelly presented her with the certificate and thanked her for her generosity. Her husband was up there, too, nodding and smiling.

The students clapped politely for them, and the school newspaper's photographer, as well as one from the local paper, took photos. The TV camera totally missed it, because they were backstage interviewing some of the girls from Saint Helen's. I hoped Mom didn't notice the omission.

She thanked everyone, and then her husband grabbed the microphone and said a few more words. He sounded arrogant, and I wondered how we'd get along if Mom ever took me home.

Next, Esperanza from Saint Helen's took the mike. "We want to thank you for your donation," she said, nodding both at Mom and at

Kelly, Susan and I, who stood by the other side of the stage. "Saint Helen's self-esteem program helps girls who've been in tough situations, and—"

Some hissing and heckling came from somewhere in the crowd. It wasn't much, but it made her stop.

She started to speak again, and there were some suspiciously familiar barking sounds.

Josh's friends.

I mounted the stairs halfway to see where they were, but all I saw was a sea of kids.

I looked up at Esperanza. All the kids were talking now.

She cocked an eyebrow at me. She didn't look upset like sad, but more like mad.

And she beckoned me up to the stage.

I didn't want to go, but how could I not support my homie?

She beckoned to Kelly too. Kelly made a "who, me?" gesture, and we nodded. She said something to Susan and then came to stand beside us, so that Kelly and I flanked Esperanza.

The kids in the crowd got quiet.

"Listen," Esperanza said, "It's not just girls in the ghetto who put up with this crap. I have it on good evidence that guys get too physical even out here in whitey land."

The kids roared.

Kelly waved her hands. "Stop it!" she yelled. "You know it's true."

And because everybody liked Kelly, they did quiet down.

"Anyway," said Esperanza, "we wanted to invite all you girls to a self-defense class we're setting up at the Asian Arts Academy in Pittsburgh."

"Sometimes you just have to know where to kick," I added with a "so there" look at Josh.

Some slow clapping started, and then a little more.

Then Susan came to the microphone. "All of you made a contribution to this effort," she said. "You sacrificed your corsages and you donated money to help girls who get in a tight spot. We want to thank you.

"I want to thank my daughters, too," she said. She held out an arm to Kelly, who grinned and went back up onstage.

"Both my daughters," Susan said, holding out a hand to me. "Come here, Trinity."

She was looking at me with the kind of fond, motherly approval I'd longed for all my life. It felt great. But it also confused me. One, because she'd just called me her daughter in front of my real mom. And two, she'd just named my name, ensuring that my real mom would know exactly who I was.

"I think it's safe to say that you've brought a whole new dimension and culture to Linden Falls and Linden High in the short time you've been here," Susan continued. The crowd clapped and a few guys yelled out some things I couldn't understand. "I know it hasn't been easy for you, but we're glad you're here."

I felt her arm around me and heard a few cheers from the student body, and it was weird. In a way, it was what I'd wanted from the Fall Queen nomination. I was getting celebrated, and I stood next to a proud mother on the stage.

But of course, it wasn't happening the way I'd planned.

And as we walked off the stage and everyone started breaking up into groups and the music started playing and the whole thing turned into a regular school dance, I couldn't decide how to feel.

The big question was, how did my mom feel?

The TV reporter came rushing up to Susan, Kelly, and me. "We'd like to do a feature on your event," she said breathlessly. "Can you sit for an interview now?"

I lifted my hands like stop signs. "Not right now. I'm ready to relax and do some dancing."

Behind me, I heard her voice. Mom's voice. "You might be interested to know that I'm making a major donation to Saint Helen's."

The reporter looked over my shoulder. I turned around.

And there we were, finally face-to-face. She was looking at me with an odd smile.

In a way, it looked like she was trying to impress me. In another way, it looked like her usual craving for publicity and attention.

Her husband had her by the elbow and was trying to turn her away. "Don't be rash," he said. "There's no need to give all our hard-earned money to those nig—"

"Hector!"

"Those future welfare queens."

Nice.

The reporter ended up doing short interviews with all of us, including my mom and Susan. I don't even know what I said. I was dazed, mad, sad, and happy all at the same time.

Mom and I kept glancing at each other and then away while the interviews went on. I wanted to talk to her, but I felt like I'd made all the moves up to this point. It was her turn.

As the reporters packed up, she shooed away her husband and came over. "Trinity, I can't believe this," she said. "Did you know, when Kelly called me, who I was?"

"It was me who called," I admitted. Now that we were actually together and talking, I felt weird. I'd wanted this for so long. I'd dreamed that once I was with her, everything would be perfect.

But now that we were together, it was all coming back to me. How I'd never been the most important person in her life.

She studied me with amazement on her face. "You were the one who called?" she asked. "But how did you find me? And why?"

"Why?" I said. "Because you're my mom."

She looked at me like she didn't get it.

"Every kid wants their mom, right?"

She didn't say anything, but a whole movie of expressions crossed her face: sadness, guilt, resentment.

I rushed to fill the awkward silence. "And besides, I wanted to impress you. I was hoping to get elected Fall Queen, but obviously, that didn't happen."

That part had been anticlimactic. The Fall King and Queen had been crowned while we were being interviewed. It was Josh and his cheerleader girlfriend. No big surprise.

"Well," Mom said, "you did something great, raising money for the girls and all."

She was praising me, but it felt empty.

All of a sudden, I got mad. "I was raising money for girls like me," I said. "Girls whose families left them at a place like Saint Helen's and never came back." I thought of the little girl I'd seen there, the one who wouldn't talk. I thought of waiting on that doorstep in the rain. "Don't you know what that does to a kid? Don't you care?"

She took a step backward. "Whoa, Trinity. I don't want to get into this. If I'd known you were here and going to bring this up . . ."

"You never would have come. That's why I changed my name when I talked to you." As I said it, I realized it was true. I'd always known I'd have to trick Mom into seeing me. Always known she didn't really want to.

What did that say about me? About her?

"Look how well you've done without me," she said. "You're fine, just fine. Look at her." She pointed to Susan, talking and laughing with the other parent chaperones and a couple of teachers. "She calls you her daughter."

I did look at Susan. And then I looked back at my mom. I thought about all I'd learned from the ALT-LIVES site. "You've done better without me, too," I said, hearing the hurt and bitterness in my voice.

"My life isn't picture-perfect," she said. "I have all kinds of problems."

I realized I didn't want to hear about them. I was supposed to be her daughter, not her shrink. She should be asking about *my* problems. "Hey, why don't you introduce me to your husband?" I asked with a big, innocent smile. "He seems like a real nice guy. Call him over here."

She shushed me. "I can't do that and you know it."

"Why not, Mom?" I asked loudly.

"Don't say that!" She actually raised a hand to cover my mouth, looking behind her to see if anyone had heard.

I pushed her hand away and shook my head.

"You know, I've wasted a lot of time wondering what was wrong with me that you didn't want me. But now I see things differently."

"We can get together once in a while," she said in a low voice. "I just can't let him know, that's all. He's, you know, not too big on . . ."

"Niggers?" I said.

She lifted her hands, palms up. "I'd like to see you."

I pictured us meeting secretly in cheap diners or anonymous hotel lobbies. What would be the point?

"That's okay," I said. "You were right before. I *am* doing fine without you." And even though my stomach did a weird little jump, I turned away.

"C'mon, Trinity!" Esperanza and another girl from Saint Helen's grabbed my hands and tried to tug me toward the dance floor. "You gotta see these foreign guys dance. We're trippin', man!"

I gave my mom a glance over my shoulder. She looked kind of pitiful, staring after me. "I'll call you," I said, and then let the girls pull me out onto the dance floor.

As I started dancing, looking around at all the black, Latino, and Asian kids getting down at white old Linden High, I felt proud. I'd done something. Like Susan said, I'd had an impact on this place.

"Hey, my little dumpling," growled someone behind me, hot breath on my neck.

Chills ran all the way through me as I turned to see Lonnie. Good chills.

"Would you dance with me?" he asked, holding out his arms.

Oh, wow, did I want to. "What about Kelly?" I asked.

He pointed off to where she was dancing with a totally gorgeous soccer player. "She's found a friend," he said.

"So have I," I said, and put my arms around him.

If you liked this book, then you'll love

MY ABNORMAL
LIFE

by Lee McClain

Turn the page for a sneak preview!

Chapter One

Okay, so maybe it wasn't such a great idea, convincing my retarded sister Danielle to hide in the back of an Ethan Allen furniture truck.

But as I hunched on the bottom porch step of a strange house in a strange town on a damp January day, it was the best escape plan I could manage.

Nothing had gone right since social services had stuck their collective noses into our lives one week ago. This was the worst yet. I'd been asked to wait outside while Dani got settled in her new home.

Without me.

That was when I saw the truck and heard the furniture movers complaining that their next stop was all the way in the middle of Pittsburgh.

Where me, Dani, and Mom lived. Hmmmm.

The seed of my big idea planted itself in my mind, and I stood up and strolled closer to the truck, keeping my eyes down, making myself as invisible as I could.

Behind me, the door to Dani's new home burst open and a guy my age slammed out onto the front porch. "Don't pay any attention to what I want, you never do!" he yelled.

The door closed behind him.

Even I, Miss Zero Experience, could see the boy was sexy. He had these broad, powerful shoulders and dark brown hair that curled over the sheepskin collar of his coat.

And, oh my gosh, his eyes. I mean, I have brown eyes, but like everything else about me, they're ordinary and forgettable.

This boy's brown eyes looked like melted chocolate. They drooped down at the outside corners, like he was just a little bit sleepy. But there was nothing sleepy about the athletic way he took the porch steps in one leap and strode down the walk.

I hadn't been this close to a good-looking boy in forever. Mostly I'd just watched them out our apartment window, or on TV. So I got a disloyal flash of thinking, "Hey, maybe it won't be so bad in this town" as I watched him come toward me.

"Why can't you people solve your own problems?" he yelled in my direction.

My warm, fuzzy feeling evaporated. "Us people? Excuse me?" I marched toward him, ready to fight. I may be short but I'm strong.

His cell phone rang, and he turned away like I wasn't even there. "Yeah?" he said into it. "Oh, just another Little Orphan Annie my folks have taken in. I was supposed to be home to, quote, make her feel welcome, but I'm bailin'."

"We're *not* orphans," I protested to his broad back.

Just at that moment, Dani came out onto the porch. She was crying with her mouth wide open, loud wails that reached into my chest and hooked my heart.

I ran up the steps and wrapped my arms around her. "Hey, it's okay," I said, even though it wasn't. I stroked her tangled, light brown hair and patted her bony back.

Her wails slowed, then stopped. "I not stay here," she said, her voice shaky. "I stay *you*."

My point exactly. I looked up at the screen door of the house, where our social worker, Fred, and the new foster mom stood watching.

"You can visit each other," Fred said.

"After she has a few days to settle in." The foster mom crossed her arms over her chest. Her chin was pointy like a witch's. "You need to tell her it's okay for her to stay here."

"You want me to lie?" I said it quietly so that Dani, whose head was now buried in my shoulder, wouldn't hear.

The foster mom's lips tightened. "Say your

goodbyes," she said. "Fred, we need to nail down some details."

The two of them disappeared back into the house.

Dani clung to me. "I stay *you*," she repeated over and over.

Her words tore at my heart, and what made it worse was that it was all my fault. If I hadn't tried to shoplift food from a new store whose owner I didn't know, the police would never have found out how Dani, Mom and I were living.

Stupid, stupid, stupid.

It was bad enough being taken away from Mom, not to mention my apartment and my neighborhood and everything I knew. But I'd thought Dani and I could stay together. Putting us in separate homes in the same small town was the brainstorm of our counselors at St. Helen's Home for Girls.

After knowing us for all of one week, they'd decided I was overly responsible and prematurely adult. And they thought Dani, at eight, was too attached to me.

Well, duh. What choice did we have?

And what was so bad about being responsible and attached?

So now, just because I'd answered some questions wrong in their interviews, I couldn't stay with Dani and help her get used to a new place.

She'd be on her own, and she did *not* handle change well.

My Grandma's words came back to me: "You're this baby's guardian angel," she'd said when Dani was born with Down's Syndrome. "With the Good Lord's help, you have to keep her safe, whatever your mother and father do."

Well, Gram, I thought, looking up toward heaven, *you better tell the Good Lord to step in quick.*

Dani wrapped herself around me like a monkey, and I carried her down the porch stairs.

And there sat the truck, open and unattended. The back of it was half full of furniture. The delivery guys were inside the next-door neighbors' house.

"Hey Dani," I said, "want to play a game?"

She lifted her head. "What game?"

I dug a used tissue out of my jeans pocket and wiped her nose. "See that truck?" I said. "We're gonna play hide-and-seek in it."

"We going 'way?" she asked.

Sometimes Dani was smarter than she looked. "That's right," I said, glancing back at the still-empty doorway of Dani's new foster home. "We're gonna go away. Hold on."

I scrambled up the ramp that led into the back of the truck and looked around. There were a couple of big dressers we could hide behind, and some green padded blankets to pull over the top of us. Perfect!

"Hey," said a voice outside the truck.

I froze.

"Are you crazy? What're you doing?"

Slowly, I turned around.

It was Mr. Sexy. "I gotta go," he said into his cell phone, and stuffed it in the pocket of his windbreaker. "Get outta there," he said to me. "Any minute now, they're going to shut this truck and drive off. You can't play in there."

I put Dani down but kept my hands on her shoulders to soothe her. "We're not playing," I said.

He came closer, hoisting himself up to sit on the back of the truck. "My mom's gonna kill you. She's super safety conscious."

"Look, just get out of here before somebody sees you," I hissed. "We're taking care of our own problems, okay? We're trying to go back home."

"You're stowing away?" He sounded the slightest bit impressed.

"It dark in here," Dani said.

"I know. We're playing cave." It was a game we played whenever the lights got turned off at home.

Dani started to cry. "I no like cave!"

I sighed. "Look," I said, kneeling down to face her, "we're going to go for a ride in this truck. A long ride, but I'll be right here with you all the time. And when it opens up again, we'll be back home."

"Are you out of your mind?" asked the boy.

"Just get out of here so nobody sees you," I snapped. "This isn't your business."

"Brian!" a woman's voice called. "Did you see where Dani and her sister went?"

I heard more people coming this way. "Off the truck, kid," said a male voice. "We're heading out."

I put my hands together to pantomime a prayer to the kid. And then I had to focus on Dani. "Come on, down here," I whispered, and pulled her behind the biggest dresser with me. "Look, we'll put this blanket over us. Be real quiet!"

A big sliding door came down, blocking all the light from the back of the truck.

The engine rumbled to life.

Dani started crying again.

As the truck started moving, I hugged her tight and tried to feel good about getting away. I'd always taken care of our family. Usually, though, I had a little more time to sort through alternatives and make a plan. This time I'd made a snap decision.

Sometimes being responsible sucks. Because what if you make a really big mistake?

At least we're together. I hugged Dani tighter. *And we're away from that mean foster mom*.

The truck screeched to a halt. Angry voices raged outside.

"What that man talk about?" Dani asked me.

"Sssh." I put my hand over her mouth, but gently so she wouldn't get mad. "We're playing a game, remember? We have to be really quiet."

"I no like cave!" she said, still crying a little.

The back of the truck opened with a screechy, metal-on-metal sound, and light flooded in.

"Anybody back here?" a man's voice called.

"Well, they're hardly likely to answer you," came the foster mom's witchy voice.

Dani jumped out of my grip. "Here we are!" she crowed.

Caught!

I let my head sink down into my hand for one tiny moment. Then, slowly, I stood up and walked out into view.

Dani danced around, all happy, thinking the game was over and she'd won. The foster mom lit into the furniture guys for not checking their truck.

Fred, the social worker, studied me. "What were you thinking?" he asked quietly. "You could have gotten hurt, or lost, at the very least. And it's not just you, it's your sister in question."

I bit my lip and looked away. He was right, and I knew it.

My eyes landed on the foster brother, Mr. Sexy. "You told," I accused him, glad to focus my anger outside of myself. "You ran to Mommy and told."

He lifted his hands. "It wasn't me. I was ready to let you go."

"Yeah, right."

He nodded toward Fred. "It was that guy. He's weird. It's like he could see you through the truck. He knew right away where you went."

"Maybe he just has a lot of experience with how deceitful young people can be," said the foster mom. Apparently she'd finished with the furniture guys and was turning her scolding tongue on us.

"Come on out, girls," Fred said, and Dani, little traitor that she was, ran to him. He helped her off the back of the truck.

I got down on my own—nobody was rushing to give *me* a hand—and right away the foster mom got on my case. "You endangered your sister. I had my reservations about you before, considering the shape she's in, but now I'm certain you're a bad influence."

I'm not normally a crier, but that remark on top of everything else just about knocked me out.

All I'd done for eight years was take care of Dani. And now this stranger had the nerve to tell me I'd done a bad job?

What was worse, I was afraid she was right.

Tears pushed at the back of my eyes and my throat started hurting.

Mr. Sexy must have noticed. "Mom, lighten up," he said.

She spun around. "You're just as bad, Brian," she snapped. "You saw them get into that truck and didn't tell me. If anything had happened, it would have been your fault. And with all your gifts, you should know better."

Brian's head dropped and he turned around. "I don't want 'em here anyway," he muttered as he walked away.

Through my misery I wondered about his so-called gifts. What were they? Or was being born normal in a household of retarded kids considered a gift in itself?

"Come on," Fred said to me. "We're late. We have to get you settled in your new home, and I know your foster parents are eager to meet you."

I dreaded the thought.

"Dani, let's go get a snack," said the foster mom.

My little sister loved food. She turned and followed the woman toward the house.

"Bye, Dani," I called with a little crack in my voice. "See you soon."

"No contact for two weeks," said the foster mom over her shoulder, looking at Fred, "and I won't report this little incident to the agency."

Two weeks? But there was so much I hadn't told the witch about Dani. How to get her to take a bath. How *Sesame Street* always calmed her down. How she liked to be sung to sleep.

My chest felt empty, like someone had pulled my heart out of it. I took a step toward Dani and the foster mom.

Fred put an arm around me and guided me toward his old beater of a car. "It'll be good for you girls to settle into your own homes," he said. "I know the Johnsons want to get you involved in some school activities."

School activities? That was the *last* thing I wanted to think about.

"Great," I said, not bothering to hide my sarcasm. I was too busy trying to hide my tears.

Amy Kaye

THE REAL DEAL

Focus on *THIS!*

Caught on tape: The newest reality television series goes on location somewhere truly dangerous—high school. Outrageous and unscripted, each episode exposes the sickest gossip, finds the facts behind the rumors, and bares the raw truth. Tune in and take it all in, because no subject is too taboo, no secret too private, and no behavior off limits!

Meet Fiona O'Hara—stuck in a suburban sitcom a million light-years away from her native New York City, a.k.a. civilization. Her mom is a basket case since the divorce. Her dad is Mr. Disappearo. And the one guy who seems like a decent love-interest has a psycho wannabe girlfriend who's ready to put a hit out on her.

THE REAL DEAL

Unscripted

Amy Kaye

Thanks to the reality-TV show that records her junior year in excruciating detail, Claire Marangello gets her big break: her own version of the TV show and a starring role in a Broadway musical. Plus Jeb, a way-hot co-star who seems to like her *that* way, and a half sister she didn't know she had. It's everything she's ever dreamed of.

Or is it a total nightmare? Her sister seems to be drifting away. Claire's not sure she can trust Jeb and his weird celebrity-centered world. The director seems to hate her; the dance steps are harder than she'd ever imagined. Claire's about to learn that while being a Broadway star is a challenge, real life has twists and turns harder than any onstage choreography and is totally . . . *UNSCRIPTED*.

YOU ARE *SO* CURSED!

NAOMI NASH

High school's a dog eat dog world, but Vickie Marotti has an edge. Scorned by the jocks and cheerleaders? Misunderstood by the uptight vice principal? No problem. Not when you're an adept street magician, hexing bullies who dare harass you or your outcast friends!

But then cute and popular upperclassman Gio Carson recognizes the truth: Vick's no more a witch than she is class president. Her dark curses are nothing more than smoke and mirrors. Will he tell the world, or will it be their little secret? Vick's about to learn a valuable lesson: that real magic lies in knowing your true friends.

The Year My Life Went Down the Loo
by Katie Maxwell

Subject: The Grotty and the Fabu (No, it's not a song.)
From: Mrs.Oded@btelecom.co.uk
To: Dru@seattlegrrl.com

Things That Really Irk My Pickle About Living in England

- The school uniform
- Piddlington-on-the-weld (I will forever be known as Emily from *Piddlesville*)
- Marmite (It's yeast sludge! GACK!)
- The ghost in my underwear drawer (Spectral hands fondling my bras—enough said!)
- No malls! What are these people *thinking???*

Things That Keep Me From Flying Home to Seattle for Good Coffee

- Aidan (*Hunkalicious!*)
- Devon (*Droolworthy?* Understatement of the year!*)
- Fang (He puts the *num* in *nummy!*)
- Holly (Any girl who hunts movie stars with me—and Oded Fehr *will be mine*—is a friend for life.)
- Über-coolio Polo Club (Where the snogging is FINE!)

They Wear WHAT Under Their Kilts?

by Katie Maxwell

Subject: Emily's Glossary for People Who Haven't Been to Scotland
From: Mrs.Legolas@kiltnet.com
To: Dru@seattlegrrl.com

Faffing about: running around doing nothing. In other words, spending a month supposedly doing work experience on a Scottish sheep farm, but really spending days on Kilt Watch at the nearest castle.

Schottie: Scottish Hottie, also known as Ruaraidh.

Mad schnoogles: the British way of saying big smoochy kisses. Will admit it sounds v. smart to say it that way.

Bunch of yobbos: a group of mindless idiots. In Scotland, can also mean sheep.

Stooshie: uproar, as in, "If Holly thinks she can take Ruaraidh from me without causing a stooshie, she's out of her mind!"

Sheep dip: not an appetizer.

What's French For "EW!"?
KATIE MAXWELL

Subject: Emily's Handy Phrases For Spring Break in Paris
From: Em-the-enforcer@englandrocks.com
To: Dru@seattlegrrl.com

J'apprendrais par coeur plutôt le Klingon qu'essaye d'apprendre le français en deux semaines.
I would rather memorize Klingon than try to learn French in two weeks.

Vous voulez que je mange un escargot?
You want me to *EAT* a snail?!?

Vous êtes nummy, mais mon petit ami est le roi des hotties, et il vient à Paris seulement pour me voir!
You are nummy, but my boyfriend is the king of hotties, and he's coming to Paris just to see me!

Didn't want this book to end?

There's more waiting at **www.smoochya.com**:

Win FREE books and makeup!
Read excerpts from other books!
Chat with the authors!
Horoscopes!
Quizzes!